MW01673887

ALL THE LIES

CHARLOTTE BYRD

CHARLOTTE BYRD

Copyright © 2020 by Charlotte Byrd, LLC.

All rights reserved.

Proofreaders:

Julie Deaton, Deaton Author Services, https://www.facebook.com/jdproofs/

Renee Waring, Guardian Proofreading Services, https://www.facebook.com/GuardianProofreadingServices

Savanah Cotton, Cotton's Incision Editing, https://www.facebook.com/Cottons-Incision-Editing-512917856115256/

Cover Design: Charlotte Byrd

No part of this book may be reproduced in any form or by any electronic or mechanical means, including information storage and retrieval systems, without written permission from the author, except for the use of brief quotations in a book review.

This book is a word of fiction. Names, characters, places, and incidents are either products of the author's imagination or are used fictitiously. Any resemblance to actual persons, living or dead, events, or locales is entirely coincidental. The author acknowledges the trademarked status and trademark owners of various products referenced in this work of fiction, which have been used without permission. The publication/use of these trademarks is not authorized, associated with, or sponsored by the trademark owners.

Visit my website at www.charlotte-byrd.com

Created with Vellum

PRAISE FOR CHARLOTTE BYRD

"BEST AUTHOR YET! Charlotte has done it again! There is a reason she is an amazing author and she continues to prove it! I was definitely not disappointed in this series!!" ★★★★★

"LOVE!!! I loved this book and the whole series!!! I just wish it didn't have to end. I am definitely a fan for life!!! ★★★★★

"Extremely captivating, sexy, steamy, intriguing, and intense!" ★★★★★

"Addictive and impossible to put down." ★★★★★

"What a magnificent story from the 1st book through book 6 it never slowed down always surprising the reader in one way or the other. Nicholas and Olive's paths crossed in a most unorthodox way and that's how their story begins it's exhilarating with that nail biting suspense that keeps you riding on the edge the whole series. You'll love it!" ★★★★★

"What is Love Worth. This is a great epic ending to this series. Nicholas and Olive have a deep connection and the mystery surrounding the deaths of the people he is accused of murdering is to be read. Olive is one strong woman with deep convictions. The twists, angst, confusion is all put together to make this worthwhile read." ★★★★★

"Fast-paced romantic suspense filled with twists and turns, danger, betrayal, and so much more." ★★★★★

"Decadent, delicious, & dangerously addictive!" - Amazon Review ★★★★★

"Titillation so masterfully woven, no reader can resist its pull. A MUST-BUY!" - Bobbi Koe, Amazon Review ★★★★★

"Captivating!" - Crystal Jones, Amazon Review ★★★★★

"Sexy, secretive, pulsating chemistry…" - Mrs. K, Amazon Reviewer ★★★★★

"Charlotte Byrd is a brilliant writer. I've read loads and I've laughed and cried. She writes a balanced book with brilliant characters. Well done!" -Amazon Review ★★★★★

"Hot, steamy, and a great storyline." - Christine Reese ★★★★★

"My oh my....Charlotte has made me a fan for life." - JJ, Amazon Reviewer ★★★★★

"Wow. Just wow. Charlotte Byrd leaves me speechless and humble… It definitely kept me on the edge of my seat. Once you pick it up, you won't put it down." - Amazon Review ★★★★★

" Intrigue, lust, and great characters...what more could you ask for?!" - Dragonfly Lady ★★★★★

WANT TO BE THE FIRST TO KNOW ABOUT MY UPCOMING SALES, NEW RELEASES AND EXCLUSIVE GIVEAWAYS?

Sign up for my newsletter: https://www.subscribepage.com/byrdVIPList

Join my Facebook Group: https://www.facebook.com/groups/276340079439433/

Bonus Points: Follow me on BookBub and Goodreads!

ABOUT CHARLOTTE BYRD

Charlotte Byrd is the bestselling author of romantic suspense novels. She has sold over 700,000 books and has been translated into five languages.

She lives near Palm Springs, California with her husband, son, and a toy Australian Shepherd who hates water. Charlotte is addicted to books and Netflix and she loves hot weather and crystal blue water.

Write her here:

charlotte@charlotte-byrd.com

Check out her books here:

www.charlotte-byrd.com

Connect with her here:

www.facebook.com/charlottebyrdbooks

www.instagram.com/charlottebyrdbooks

www.twitter.com/byrdauthor

Sign up for my newsletter: https://www.subscribepage.com/byrdVIPList

Join my Facebook Group: https://www.facebook.com/groups/276340079439433/

Bonus Points: Follow me on BookBub and Goodreads!

facebook.com/charlottebyrdbooks
twitter.com/byrdauthor
instagram.com/charlottebyrdbooks
bookbub.com/profile/charlotte-byrd

ALSO BY CHARLOTTE BYRD

All books are available at ALL major retailers! If you can't find it, please email me at charlotte@charlotte-byrd.com

The Perfect Stranger Series

The Perfect Stranger

The Perfect Cover

The Perfect Lie

The Perfect Life

The Perfect Getaway

The Perfect Couple

All the Lies Series

All the Lies

All the Secrets
All the Doubts
All the Truths
All the Promises
All the Hopes

Tell me Series

Tell Me to Stop
Tell Me to Go
Tell Me to Stay
Tell Me to Run
Tell Me to Fight
Tell Me to Lie

Wedlocked Trilogy

Dangerous Engagement
Lethal Wedding
Fatal Wedding

Tangled Series

Tangled up in Ice
Tangled up in Pain
Tangled up in Lace
Tangled up in Hate
Tangled up in Love

Black Series

Black Edge

Black Rules

Black Bounds

Black Contract

Black Limit

Not into you Duet

Not into you

Still not into you

Lavish Trilogy

Lavish Lies

Lavish Betrayal

Lavish Obsession

Standalone Novels

Dressing Mr. Dalton

Debt

Offer

Unknown

ALL THE LIES

To save my job, I have to get an interview with a reclusive bestselling author who is impossible to find.

It's an insurmountable task until I get a lead. It's probably a joke but given what just happened in my personal life, it's an excuse to get away.

The last person I expect to see there is ***him*, the dashing and mysterious stranger** who was the only man who knew the truth *that* night.

He invites me inside under one condition: everything he says is off the record. He'll answers my questions but I can't write about him.

Then things get even more complicated.

Something happens between us.

His touch ignites a spark. His eyes make me weak at the knees.

We can't do this.

But then he looks at me in that way that no one has ever looked at me and I can't say no…

1

EMMA

"You either get this done or you're fired," my boss says, slamming the door to my office in my face.

A cold shiver runs down my spine.

This is an impossible task.

It's also a trap.

She knows that I could never get an interview with someone like D. B. Carter and it's her way of finally getting rid of me.

I put my head on my desk and sob. I've never cried at work before.

I've always saved those moments of total breakdown for the couch in my living room where I could have a glass of wine in one hand and a remote in the other, but today I just can't stop myself.

Corrin Matthews has been trying to get rid of me for months. She's my immediate superior and she has made my life at Coast Magazine impossible.

She's the kind of boss who never lets up. She works harder than everyone else and is always the first one to get to the office and the last to leave.

It's not that I'm not a hard worker. It's just that I do my best work outside of here.

After a while, the walls start to feel like they're closing in and I need to grab my laptop and write somewhere else.

I hope that it doesn't seem like I'm slacking, but I think it does.

Of course, it doesn't help that there's something else creating the wedge between us; my fiancé.

Tall, easy on the eyes, and broad-shouldered, Alex Wetterling first bought Corrin a drink during a girls' night out after work.

When she went to the bathroom, he bought me one, too, and we ended up closing down the bar, driving to Zuma Beach, and making out in the front seat until the sun came up.

He was quite a gentleman that night and for three more dates after and we did nothing more than kiss, laugh, and talk.

After wiping my eyes, I call Alex on the phone, but he doesn't answer. I know that he can't always talk on the phone while at work. I text him a couple of times, but he doesn't reply.

I turn on the camera on my phone and check my appearance. My eyes are bloodshot. I dab a little concealer underneath and hope that's enough to cover up the evidence of tears.

Everyone in the office knows that Corrin hates my guts and many have even admitted it out loud. I wish there was something I could do to change it, but I can't.

Corrin's uncle owns Coast, this fledgling magazine trying to compete in an ultra-competitive environment where print and online media outlets with much more power and gravitas go under all the time.

Coast started out as something of a

lifestyle magazine focusing on coastal living and showcasing brands that represent that style.

However, when one of the writers broke a story about a movie studio executive abusing many well-known actresses and other female executives, Coast found something of a niche in juicy investigative journalism.

Daniel Matthews, Corrin's uncle, was very keen to jump on all of this exposure and even found a few journalists from other news outlets to do deep dive pieces similar to this one.

Back at the University of Southern California's School of Journalism, I wrote a number of pieces for the school's newspaper that got picked up by the LA Times.

My stories focused on the sexual abuse that the head gynecologist perpetrated against female students for almost three decades.

USC had paid the students settlements in a number of these cases to keep quiet and I almost didn't get my degree in my efforts to uncover the truth.

It was Daniel Matthews who conducted my interview and who hired me on the spot. When he had a heart attack and had to take time off, his niece, Corrin Matthews, increased her sphere of influence.

Now she is the managing news director and in charge of my entire department.

It would be a stretch to say that Corrin is bad at her job.

She isn't. Actually, she's quite good.

The problem is that she can't stand the sight of me and despite how good she wants Coast to be, she's going to do everything in her power to stop me from making a career here.

"Alex, pick up. I know you're there. I really need to talk to you," I speak into my watch on the way to his office and it sends the text message.

We don't have plans to meet until our engagement party tonight, but his office is only five blocks away from mine in downtown LA and I know that he's going to be on his lunch break soon.

I stop into Just Thai and order two of our favorites to go and text him again. It's not like him to ignore my texts, so I actually get worried that something might've happened.

Alex and I have been together for two years today. We decided to hold our engagement party tonight, on a Thursday, because it is our two year anniversary. We both took tomorrow off to have a little staycation in Laguna Beach in celebration of our impending nuptials.

I'm not much of a party planner, so my mom and sisters are taking care of all the details. My parents are even hosting it at their Calabasas home, which is tucked in the hills above Malibu.

My phone rings.

I answer immediately and then realize that it's Lindsey, my very helpful, but often annoying, sister.

She's three years older than I am, married and expecting her first child with her husband, who is an attorney in my father's firm. While I have always been somewhat of a tomboy, favoring the color black and refusing to wear a dress even to prom, Lindsey is totally Blair from *The Facts of Life*.

She has never encountered a pink that she did not like and her room, growing up, always looked like a bottle of Pepto-Bismol had exploded in it. Her style matured in her twenties and now she always shows up so stylish and put together that I feel like she is walking out of an issue of Vogue.

"Listen," Lindsey starts talking as soon as I answer. "This is an emergency. The caterer has totally flaked and now we have no idea what to do."

My mouth drops open.

I shake my head and stare at my reflection in the mirror on the counter.

The front desk woman hands me my boxes of food and hungry patrons usher me out of the door.

"What do you mean?" I ask.

"That's exactly what I mean. We didn't want to worry you, but it happened this morning and Mom and I are trying to find someone else. So far, we haven't had much luck."

“I'm really sorry,” I say after a long pause.

I know that I should be more concerned, but if it were up to me, I wouldn't even be having an engagement party. It was really Alex's idea to have this big bash and to bring the families together so that they can meet each other before the actual wedding.

“No,” Lindsey says. “I'm the one that’s sorry. I found that stupid caterer and a few celebrities had used her so I thought that she was reliable, but just because you have been written up in Cosmo doesn't mean shit. Sorry about my language.”

Lindsey is the kind of girl who curses like a sailor but then apologizes like a church lady, as if there is anyone in the room who hasn’t heard that word before.

“Lindsey, *don't* worry about it,” I say as calmly as possible. “You’re six months pregnant. You really shouldn't be getting all worked up about this.”

“How can you be so calm?” she gasps in frustration. “Agh. I knew that I shouldn’t have called you. Mom and I will deal with it. Don’t worry.”

She hangs up before I get a chance to say another word. I stare at the phone as I wave hello to Larry, the security guard in Alex's building, and then wait for the elevator.

After all these years, I'm pretty used to getting railroaded when it comes to parties and other family gatherings by my mom and by my sisters.

2

EMMA

The inside of the elevator is all glass and looks out onto the skyscrapers of LA. The city is sprawling and big, but most of the buildings are about two or three stories. The tall, massive ones are concentrated in the downtown area.

I ride all the way to the 18th floor in this silent elevator while my thoughts return to the impossible interview. Corrin wants me to interview D. B. Carter, who is as reclusive a writer as there is one.

For one thing, no one even knows what he looks like. For another, I'm not even entirely sure if he is even a man.

Since I don't know the sex, I'll refer to him as him for now. So much for smashing the patriarchy, right?

D. B. Carter is an international best-selling author of a very popular fantasy series.

He is prolific, with over a hundred books and perhaps even more titles if you count all the novellas, short stories, and standalone novels he has written in his life.

The other thing that's particularly interesting about him is that he's independently published.

He doesn't have a publisher so he has been self-publishing all of his work. He has a strong social media presence, but nothing personal is ever posted.

Of course, there are no pictures.

There is also no personal information of any kind. Many authors will state the city and state or country where they live. They might mention a spouse, children, or pets. None of these details exist about D. B. Carter.

I know this because I have looked.

Unfortunately, it was my idea to write

about D. B. Carter in the first place. A friend of mine mentioned that he was her favorite author. When I looked him up, I saw how well he was selling on Amazon and other platforms.

I tried to find out more about him, but I couldn't. When I downloaded his book onto my Kindle, I realized what all the fuss was about.

I couldn't stop turning the pages.

I was addicted.

I stayed up half the night reading and the funny thing is that I don't even really like fantasy. There was something about the characters, the setting, and his use of language that lured me in and kept me there until I was done.

I'm a journalist and we like to think that we are objective. Of course, there is no such thing. We all come with our innate and implicit biases that guide the stories that we choose to tell and how we tell those stories.

When I was at that pitch meeting, sitting behind that Formica table with my colleagues listening to Corrin rant about taking the magazine to the next level, I didn't have any other ideas. But I had just stayed up the whole night reading his book and couldn't wait to start the next one. What made him particularly interesting was that he was a bigger mystery than I had even envisioned.

The box of Thai food feels warm against my stomach and it calms my nerves somewhat. I can't wait to talk to Alex about this impossible assignment.

I have no idea where to start.

In this day and age, every search begins online, but outside of his books, he barely exists.

It reminds me of that old saying, if a tree falls in the forest and no one is there to hear it fall, did it actually happen?

If a person doesn't exist on the Internet, does he actually exist at all?

Alex's office is at the far end of the hallway from the elevators. He is an associate at his father's boutique investment bank.

It's not a particularly big enterprise in that it doesn't have that many employees, but it's very profitable. Mr. Wetterling is very careful about keeping costs down and staying below the number of employees that he needs to remain a small business even though the firm made almost five hundred million in profit last year.

There are only a couple of office assistants; one who works for his father and another who answers the calls that come in for all of the associates.

I wave to the younger one and ask about her daughter who has recently been diagnosed with a kidney infection. Afterward I walk down the brightly lit modern hallway and nod to every associate with their door open.

When I finally get to Alex's office, I knock and wait.

No one answers, so I knock a little louder.

When I try the handle, the door swings open and I see Alex with his pants down, his shirt untucked, and a woman bent over his desk.

"Emma!" Alex yells, looking back at me, and trips pulling up his pants.

I straighten my back as the blood coursing through my body turns to ice.

When he moves out of my field of vision, I see *her*.

She just sits up on the desk, crosses her legs, and buttons up her tailored, dry clean-only, silk blouse.

"What's happening here?" I ask. With my palms drenched in sweat, the Thai food slips out of my hands and drops to the floor.

3

EMMA

When I look back up at them, everything moves in slow motion. Alex walks up to me and says something, but I don't hear him.

My ears buzz.

The woman my fiancé was just having sex with is his boss, Jennifer Lester.

I look past her and then stare at the giant floor-to-ceiling window behind her.

The view of the city is magnificent. Breathtaking.

Is it just this scene that is taking my breath away and tightening my chest?

I try to inhale but my throat closes up.

I turn to walk away, but Alex stops me.

He puts his hand on the door and pushes it back, shutting it.

"You can't leave," he says. "We need to talk about this."

I flip my body around. The adrenaline starts pumping through my veins and I feel myself coming back to life.

"What do you want to talk about?" I ask.

"You weren't supposed to be here," Alex says.

I shake my head.

"No," he backtracks. It's only just occurred to him that that's the wrong thing to say. "That's not what I meant. I'm sorry."

"How could you do this to me?" I ask. "Today's our engagement party."

"I know," he whispers, "I'm sorry."

"Fuck you," I say and spit on the floor.

I haven't spat like that since I played softball, but it feels visceral and good. I push past him and walk out of the office.

I'm tempted to trot, but I stop myself.

I have done nothing wrong.

I have no reason to run away.

I almost get to the elevator when Alex

catches up with me and pulls me into the empty office across from the front desk.

He closes the door behind us. The room smells like it has recently been painted. It's completely empty with nothing but a chair near the far wall.

"Where are you going?" Alex asks.

"Away."

"Listen, I'm sorry. I had no idea you were coming."

"Yes, I know. Otherwise, you would have continued lying."

"I'm such an asshole. I know that. I've just been working so much and I've been so overwhelmed with everything. Can we talk about this?"

"How long has this been going on?" I ask, crossing my arms.

He hesitates.

"You wanted to talk so answer me."

I whip my hair around and walk over to the enormous floor-to-ceiling window. I look down at the street below and stare at the restaurant where I just got takeout at for my fiancé and contemplate how much my life has changed in the last twenty minutes.

Alex walks over to me and puts his arms around my shoulders. I brush him off, but he does it again.

"I'm really sorry, Emma. I'm such a dick. I'm such a shit-head."

"You're also a liar and a cheater," I say.

"I know."

"How long has this been going on?" I ask him again.

Again, he hesitates.

"Listen, you were the one that wanted to talk. You want to explain yourself? Then do it. Tell me the truth."

"Jen is my boss," he says.

She's also ten years older than you, I want to add, but I bite my tongue. I want to hear what he has to say.

"The truth is that, and this is really difficult to say… we have been together for a long time."

My mouth drops open. A part of me thought that this might be a one-time thing. Not that that was okay, but at least it would be…

"What are you talking about?" I ask,

feeling all the blood drain away from my face.

"Jen and I have been together since before you and I met. We've been dating for about five years."

"Dating? She's married. She has two children."

"I know, but it was just something that happened and then it kept happening. I knew that shc did not want to divorce her husband and that was okay with me. I didn't want anything serious either."

"You didn't want anything serious?" I ask. "We have been together for two years. We've been practically living together. You asked me to marry you."

"I know," Alex says. "I didn't want anything special with her. When I met you, I knew that I wanted to have a life with you."

"So why didn't you stop seeing her?" I ask and shake my head.

"I tried," he says with a shrug. "We never really saw each other outside of work. This occasional rendezvous over lunch, a few times a week, that's just something we started doing five years ago and it just continued. It never got serious and it never got past that point of just… sex. We became something like coworkers who slept together occasionally, at work."

I stare at his beautiful toned face, his luscious lips, and his thick ash blonde hair. I can't believe that this is the same person who I thought I was going to spend the rest of my life with.

Outside of our very demanding jobs, we have practically spent every minute together.

We stopped hanging out with friends and acquaintances. We missed family dinners.

We stayed up late talking into the night when we had to be up early the next day.

When I met Alex, I never thought that I would ever connect with someone like this. I never thought that there would be a person who intuitively understood every part of me. Then he came along and suddenly all of these things that I thought were important no longer were. I thought that he felt the same way.

Tears start to gather and I blink to make them go away.

A big gulp forms somewhere in the back of my throat.

I'm crying because I caught him cheating on me, but it's more than that. There's this dissipation of trust. There's this feeling that this life that you have been living for two years is nothing but a lie.

"Emma, please," Alex says, tugging on my hand. "Please don't cry. I hate to see you cry."

I pull my hand away and wipe a rogue tear with the knuckle of my index finger.

"I can't believe that you've been lying to me for so long," I say quietly. "Our whole relationship is a lie."

"No, it's not," Alex says, shaking his head.

I cock my head and look into his eyes, unconvinced.

"I know that I shouldn't have been doing this. I know that I should have cut things off with Jen a long time ago, but you have to believe me when I say that it didn't mean anything. It was just a stupid physical thing. We have been doing it for three years up until we met. I broke things off for about a year. Then we were both working late one night and it just happened again."

"So, you broke things off at first?" I ask, my voice cracking.

"Yes, when we met," Alex says urgently.

"And then when things got a little bit too boring with us, you just went right back to her?" I ask.

He reaches over to me, but I turn away from him.

This time, however, I don't just pull away. I forcibly remove his hands off of my shoulders.

"No, that's not what happened. It was just stupid. It was something we did for a while and it's just like… a bad habit."

"Well, in my opinion, cheating is not the same thing as smoking. The problem is that you never gave it a second thought about what it would do to *me*. You didn't care how much it would hurt me. You don't care about any of that."

"I did," Alex says, his voice getting more desperate. "I still do."

"No, you don't," I say with a sigh.

Before he can say another word, the

door swings open and Jen walks in. She's tall and elegant with hair that looks like she has just walked off the red carpet. On the outside, she is a much better match for Alex than I am. When Jen stands next to him, I can almost see that glitzy, airbrushed magazine photograph of the two of them, smiling with their big pearly whites from ear to ear. Hell, they would even look good on the cover of Coast.

"Emma, I just wanted to stop by and apologize. This was very disrespectful and a terrible thing to do. I'm really sorry. It should have never happened."

I give her a slight nod. As a woman who writes for a living, it is not lost on me that her veiled apology is not really an apology at all. There is a detachment, not just in her tone but also in her choice of words.

"I promise you that this will never happen again. From now on, our relationship will be strictly professional," Jen adds.

"I don't really care," I say quietly but sternly. "You can do whatever you want because I'm not going to be with someone who treats me like this."

Jen nods and looks at me with sympathy but also admiration.

I've had enough of this. I take a deep breath and walk toward the door, but when Jen reaches out and touches me with her manicured fingers, my whole body shudders.

"Don't touch me," I snap.

"Please, Emma, I'm sorry. I just have to ask you a small favor."

"You want to ask me a favor?" I parrot her words back to her, flabbergasted.

"Please don't tell anyone. This whole thing is so stupid and Alex and I should have never happened. I love my husband and my family. I don't know what I would do if I were to lose that."

Not knowing how to respond to that, I just walk out.

4

EMMA

I keep my tears at bay on the way down the elevator and in the lobby. But as soon as the brightness of the sun hits my face, all the tears come rushing out. They burst out of me and I start to suffocate. Gasping for air, I fold in half and collapse onto the ground.

Someone walks up to me and asks if I'm okay. I see his mouth moving, but I can't hear any of the words because my ears are buzzing so loudly.

"I'm fine," I keep repeating to myself over and over again.

Eventually, he leaves and others appear, walking around me, clearing me with a six-foot radius. It's almost as if whatever kind of sadness I have, they never want to experience it and would rather not look at me than confront the possibility.

When I'm able to breathe again, I force myself to my feet and then start to walk in the general direction of my office building. Frankly, I have no idea how to deal with this.

I've had girlfriends back in college get cheated on, but it never happened to me. They were upset, of course, and jealous, but I never really understood how they felt until this very moment.

I look at the ground.

Suddenly, I'm standing in quicksand. My head starts to spin and I have to lean against the wall to keep my balance. The whole world tilts on its axis because the things that I knew for certain about my life are the complete opposite of that.

I knew that I loved Alex and that Alex loved me back. I knew that he understood every part of me. I knew that he cared about me in that true way that only someone who wants to spend the rest of his life with you would care about you.

What I did not know was that Alex had a secret life.

What I did not know was that Alex was already with someone else when he met me and they stayed together after we got engaged.

He tried to explain it as if it wasn't a real relationship. She's married, and she has another life. But the truth is that he and Jen spend a hundred hours a week together.

How is that not a relationship?

She may be married, but she's also a workaholic, just like Alex.

What they've had over the past five years was probably so much more than what Alex and I had.

Take a deep breath.

Comparison is the death of joy. Mark Twain said that and he is right. I'm walking here trying to compare what Alex and I had to what he had with his boss when really it has nothing to do with any of that.

The only things that matter are that Alex lied and that our relationship was not what I thought it was. These lies cut so deep that it makes me question whether or not I can ever come up for air again.

In the meantime, my phone rings and when I look down at the screen, I see that it's Lindsey. She's probably calling with an update about tonight's festivities.

My throat closes up.

No, no, no.

This is not happening.

What the hell do I do now?

Our engagement party is in a few hours and, in addition to all the Southern California locals who have to brave rush hour traffic to get there, there are people flying in from Seattle, San Francisco, and New York.

The last time that I heard the headcount it was a little bit over 200 people. The guest list got so big that it might as well be the wedding itself, but my mom insisted that no one could be missed.

My phone rings again.

It's Alex.

I don't want to answer, but I don't know what to do about the party.

He starts talking as soon as I press the

green button, profusely apologizing for something unforgivable.

"This isn't why I answered," I interrupt. "I'm not changing my mind. But we need to discuss the party."

"What's there to talk about?" he asks after a pause.

"We have to cancel it."

"No," Alex says. "Absolutely not."

"What are you talking about? We're *not* getting married. The engagement is off."

"My parents flew all the way from New York to be here and your mom is spending thousands of dollars to host this incredible event for us. We can't just call it off and ruin everyone's night. The least we can do is show up and be there."

"Are you kidding me?" I ask, pulling the phone away from my ear and actually staring at the screen as if he has lost his mind.

"I'm not going to go to our engagement party with you after what I just walked into."

"Listen, I'm really sorry about that and I want to make it up to you, but we can't be so self-centered. We have guests flying in from all over the place to see us and to meet the family."

"There is no family," I correct him. "We are not joining our families. This whole evening will be a lie. I can't believe that I have to explain this to you."

"I know what you're saying," Alex says, carefully choosing his words. "But my family is flying in. My parents, my aunt, and my uncle. I can't just tell them that the party is off. Besides, think about your sister and your mom. They put a lot of work into planning this thing and we can't just cancel it."

"I'm not talking about this anymore," I say, shaking my head. "I can't believe that I'm actually having this conversation. I have to go back to work."

I DON'T WANT to be here. I want to go home to my apartment and cry onto my pillows. I don't want to see my coworkers, my boss, or anyone else for that matter.

But if I leave now, Corrin will

undoubtably notice and use it against me in the future.

"You're late," she says.

"I'm sorry," I mumble under my breath.

Corrin's office is one of the first ones near the elevator and it's impossible to not walk past it.

There's nothing really to say and I already feel like I'm on the verge of breaking down, so I just keep going. My cubicle is on the other side of the hallway and as soon as I see it, I duck inside and bury my head in my folded arms on my desk.

The rest of the afternoon passes in a blur. I wait out the hours by trying to distract myself with Buzzfeed, LA Times, and social media, but nothing seems to take my mind off Alex.

I look through his Instagram, focusing on the selfies that he took with Jen at all of those after work meetings I never knew they had.

Here's them at a bar in Denver.

Here's them at a coffee shop early in the morning before a big presentation for new clients in Jackson Hole.

Was Alex just with me because he couldn't have Jen all to himself?

Was he only with me because she refused to leave her husband and break up her family?

With one hour left, I go to the bathroom and call my mom. I should've called earlier, but I was too afraid that I would start crying in the middle of a phone call.

I take a deep breath and tell myself to be strong. Focused. Determined.

5

EMMA

When Mom answers the phone, I can feel the smile on her face and practically taste the excitement. All the preparations are almost done and her favorite part, the part where she gets dressed and glammed up, is about to begin.

"Mom, I have some bad news," I start. "We need to cancel the party."

"Absolutely not," she says without missing a beat.

"You don't even know what happened."

"I would like to know, but I also want you to know that I'm not canceling this party."

This takes me by surprise.

I thought she would argue with me, but I didn't realize that she would be this categorical about it.

I take a deep breath. I didn't want to come out and tell her the cold, ugly truth, but now I feel like I don't have a choice.

“I caught Alex with another woman,” I say slowly, pausing after each word. “Today. I walked in on them.”

My phone buzzes and when I look at the screen, I see that she's trying to call me over FaceTime. I don't want to see her, but I accept the call anyway.

“Does he want to be with her?” Mom asks, looking straight into my eyes.

She's sitting in a chair in her large all white bathroom and there is a woman working on styling her hair.

“He says that he's sorry. He still wants to marry me, but of course I can't.”

“Emma—” Mom begins.

I interrupt her and say, “He has been seeing her since before he met me. He's been cheating on me the whole time we have been together.”

I wasn't going to tell her this. Not any of it.

It's embarrassing.

Plus, Mom and I don't have that close of a relationship.

But what Alex did hurt me so much to my core that she has to understand that there's no way I'm going to go through with tonight.

"Emma, I'm really sorry, but I have to tell you something."

I shake my head no. I don't want to hear any of it.

"Listen to me," Mom says, bringing her phone close to her face.

She waves the hairdresser off and then says, "Men get funny about marriage. Alex has never been married before. He probably feels like his whole life is coming to an end. That's how your father felt. He cheated on me, too, before we got married. I was upset, betrayed, angry. I was everything that you are feeling right now. And you know what? I married him and I forgave him. He never cheated on me again."

I take a deep breath and exhale slowly.

I never knew that my father did that to my mother and I never knew that she forgave him for it.

Maybe he cheated on her afterward and she just doesn't know about it.

Maybe he didn't.

Either way, it's not good enough. She should know that there are people out there that won't treat her like this.

"Are you seriously telling me that I should forgive him?" I ask.

"Yes, of course."

I hate this. I hate realizing that I am profoundly disappointed in the people that I thought my parents were.

"Is it because you planned this big party and you don't want to cancel it or is it because you think that it's okay for a man to treat me like this?" I challenge her.

"No, to both of those questions. It's wrong, what he did, and of course I'm not trying to get you to make up with him just because of tonight's party. But what I want you to know is that relationships are complicated. People aren't perfect. Alex is a wonderful guy who made a mistake."

"Why are you on his side?" I ask. "What's so special about him? Why don't you want something better for me than a man who treats me like dirt?"

"That's not what I'm saying. You're putting words in my mouth, Emma, and you know it."

"I'm not going to marry Alex and we're not having this party."

"This party is costing your father and me $30,000," she says, taking a deep breath and lowering her voice to a barely audible whisper. "Lindsey and I have spent a lot of time planning every last detail and the guests are flying in from all over the US. If you don't want to marry Alex, that's your decision. But you will be there tonight and you will be polite and friendly. We are having this goddamn party."

My mouth drops open.

"So you want me to show up and just pretend that everything is fine?"

"No, not necessarily," Mom says with a smile at the corner of her lips. "If you *don't* want to pretend that everything is fine, then you are more than welcome to tell everyone how you've been humiliated by your fiancé and even go into all of the details about exactly what he did to you. I don't care what you do. But I am having this event for all of those people who have RSVP'd. I'm not canceling it. You will be there and you will be on your best behavior."

It has been a long time since my mom has talked to me like this. The last time was probably during my college graduation party. It was another party that I had no interest in having or attending, but one that she deemed absolutely necessary.

For some reason, I thought that I was grown up enough so that she didn't scare me anymore. But looking at her face on the screen, I realize that maybe certain things never go away. Her words hurt me almost as deeply as Alex's actions and yet, I still find myself wanting her support.

When the workday is finally over, I gather my things and walk over to the elevators. I try to sneak past Corrin's office, but she catches me and calls me inside.

"I expect to have an update on D. B. Carter on my desk on Monday."

"This Monday?" I ask.

"Yes, of course, this Monday. I've been assigned the story and I want regular progress reports."

I stare at her, unsure as to what to say.

"I don't know what I can have for you by Monday," I finally stutter. "He's a total recluse. I don't even know if he's a he. There's very little information about him on the Internet."

"People were able to report the news without the Internet back in the day. You are aware of that fact, right?"

I hate the attitude and the tone of her voice when she talks to me. It's like she wants to make me feel worse than I already do.

"What makes you think that I'll be able to find him or even if I do, that he'll talk to me?" I ask. "He never talks to anybody."

"You know what, Emma," Corrin says, tapping her finger on her desk while looking away from me. "You are much more capable than you give yourself credit for. You care about this job very much, so I expect you to do it."

I don't know how she does it, but for

some reason Corrin is capable of saying the most complimentary things in the most ruthless and off-putting way. Her words are drenched in sarcasm and I know that she doesn't mean a single thing that she has just said to me.

"Okay," I say, "I'll get you something by Monday."

"Great, thanks," she says with a fake smile. "Oh, by the way," she adds as I start to walk away from her, "congratulations on your engagement."

6

EMMA

When I get home, I strip off my blouse, pencil skirt, and bra and get into the shower. It feels warm and comforting, but as soon as I turn it off, I know that my day is not over. In fact, it's only just beginning.

I live in a studio apartment in downtown LA in one of those forgotten four-plexus that no one has remodeled in years.

There's no air-conditioning.

The woman who lives below me lives on social security and has five cats.

She likes to play the trumpet around nine o'clock each night, which normally would annoy me, but her cats always let me pet them so I don't complain.

It's no secret that my parents have a lot of money, but their money is not my money.

Unlike my sisters, I want to live on what I earn, but because I'm a magazine writer in 21st century America, I don't make much.

I stare out the window, looking past the bars at the bleak alleyway outside. There are No Parking signs everywhere and not a single tree in sight.

My block doesn't have many trees at all and that's not uncommon for low-income locations like this one.

In comparison to this place, Alex's brand new two-bedroom condo overlooks a park square, with mature landscaping, a few benches, and even four or five lush flowerbeds.

After our wedding, we planned to buy something together. He kept pestering me to move in with him every time I stayed over, which was almost every day.

Still, I kept this place. I don't know why. There are bars on the windows, the closet is the size of a postage stamp, and just not enough wall space for all of my books.

I pay about $1,200 a month for this crappy place and Alex pays $3,000.

He makes so much that he didn’t want me to contribute to the rent. But still something was keeping me here.

It didn't make any financial sense, but then again when has anything that I have ever done made any financial sense?

My parents wanted to pay for my school, but I chose to take out loans and make my own way in the world.

I know that my decision to do so had a lot to do with hubris and pride, but it was my choice and I wanted to see that I could do it.

I did the same thing when it came to the car. To celebrate my graduation from college, my father presented me with a brand new white BMW with all the bells and whistles, but I refused to accept it.

I had saved up for a 2012 Toyota Prius and the fact that it drove my parents crazy that I would be seen driving that car in their neighborhood in front of all their friends and acquaintances, was just a little cherry on top of the whole situation.

I open my closet door and stare at the two dresses that I have.

I bought both of them on sale at Nordstrom Rack. I don't normally shop there, but I knew given that my mom and sister were hosting this party for me that they would expect me to wear something decent.

The blue dress with the Michael Kors tag pinches at my waist. I examine my reflection in the stand-up mirror, a splurge that I had allowed myself when I saw it at West Elm and couldn't take my eyes off of it.

I rarely feel that way about things or clothing, so I figured that I could allow myself this one indulgence.

The girl looking back at me looks tired and exhausted. The makeup that I had applied earlier has washed off. My hair, shoulder-length and light brown, is half-dry and half-frizzy.

While my sisters are probably getting their hair professionally blow dried and their makeup professionally applied, I do it all myself.

I've never liked getting glammed up, especially not in a room full of relatives. I have always felt like an outsider and the girl staring back at me now confirms that fact.

I take off the blue dress and reach for the dark blue one with little pink flowers that I got at a thrift store on Fairfax Avenue.

I know that they are expecting me in something more lavish and appropriate for the evening, but the fact that I have to go there in the first place is making my blood boil.

They have worked hard on this party, but I also know that I shouldn't be expected to go to my own engagement party a few hours after I caught my fiancé cheating on me.

After I change into the thrift store dress, I look at myself in the mirror.

Yes, this is much better. The dress is casual, but not so casual that it looks like a day dress.

In a picture, it could possibly pass for something costing over $200, but up close, you can tell that the material is subpar.

I don't care.

It feels nice to the touch and it looks good on me.

Let's just say that I don't have that type of body shape that's becoming to all dresses.

That's one of the reasons that I tend to stay away from them in the first place.

I feel most comfortable in something casual; leggings, a big T-shirt, and sneakers.

Heels? I fucking hate heels.

I slip my feet into the most comfortable pair of low-rise loafers that I have and grab the heels that I'm going to wear at the party with me.

I scan the room looking for anything that I might have forgotten. Catching my reflection in the mirror again, I know that my mom will be disappointed.

I let my hair air dry without a stitch of product. I'm wearing a little bit of foundation and mascara.

My lips are lined with one of my favorite plumb colors of gloss and my eyebrows are accentuated with just a little bit of wax.

The look basically says I'm trying but not very hard.

I don't care.

I'm going there in protest.

It's the last place that I want to be, but I'm afraid that if I don't show up the consequences will be dire.

The cerebral, objective part of me realizes that given that I'm a grown woman who doesn't rely on her parents for money, there are not many consequences that they even have the ability to give me, but still.

After all these years, I feel a sense of obligation to keep up appearances and to not fuck my mom and sisters over by standing up a party in my own honor.

The last thing I grab before walking out the door is my Kindle. The walls of my apartment are lined with bookshelves which overflow with books.

I have loved to read since I was a little girl. Nothing makes me feel better about escaping into another world and into other people's problems like a good book.

When it comes to reading, I like both paper books and ebooks. I always carry my Kindle in my purse. It's small and doesn't take up much room and never weighs me down and it can hold thousands of books.

There's something different about it than just reading on my phone. This is a device just for reading. There are no interruptions and no notifications. I'm not tempted to go on social media or do anything else.

I know that it's probably a long shot that I'll be able to sneak away sometime during the party, but I take it with me just in case.

7

EMMA

After fighting traffic for close to two hours, I finally get to the hills above the 101. It's springtime and the land is green and lush after a winter soaked in rain.

As I go around the narrow switchbacks, a sweeping view of the ocean pops up, taking my breath away.

I grew up here and I pretend to like the grind and the concrete that dominates downtown LA, but I really don't.

When I pull up to the gate of my parents' sprawling estate and enter the code, my chest tightens up.

Regardless of the views or the avocado orchard that welcomes me up the curvy driveway, claustrophobia settles in.

My parents' estate is a 7,000 square-foot house in a gated community with three other homes. It sits on about 5 acres, most of which are made up of avocado, orange, and lemon groves.

I grew up in Calabasas and the city has never been that famous or popular before the Kardashians.

I also did not grow up in this house.

My parents moved here a few years ago just as I have moved into my studio apartment downtown.

While I was there for their relocation and watched my mom supervise the movers, asking them to rearrange the furniture at least three times around the living, dining, and sitting areas, neither of my parents have ever made the trip to see my apartment.

It's not that they didn't want me to move out.

They did.

They were just not pleased that I had

refused their money and insisted on living in *such a sad place*, my mom's exact phrasing.

The thing is that I sort of get it. Both of my parents grew up lower middle class. My mom got her undergraduate degree from UCLA in nursing and that's where she met my dad who ended up going to law school.

When I was growing up, we were quite well off.

Not well off by Los Angeles standards, but rather by America's and by the world's standards.

My dad made about $200,000 a year and we lived in a comfortable four bedroom house with a small pool and a big backyard.

But it was nothing like the estate that they got when he started clearing more than $3 million a year with his new clients.

I couldn't be happier for them. I know that they worked hard for every penny, but I also know that they had certain advantages other people don't.

But when it came to me?

I didn't feel comfortable taking their money, especially if I had a job that paid me a salary.

My sisters, on the other hand, had no such reservations.

When I pull up to the grand white columns out front, the valet meets me and takes the keys to my car.

Looking up at the stunning foyer with wall-to-wall marble, I wonder if I'm being an idiot for even considering getting a second job as a bartender just so that I can pay the student loan payments that are coming due in a month.

I had postponed them as much as I could, but now I have to pay almost another $1,500 a month in addition to my rent. It's the kind of money that I don't have, but it's also the kind of money that my parents wouldn't even notice.

A server approaches me as soon as I walk through the ornate double doors and hands me a glass of champagne.

One of my mom's friends from Pilates, whom I have only met on one other occasion, rushes over and gives me air kisses on both cheeks as I try to remember her name.

After we both compliment each other on

what we're wearing, however disingenuously, the server trips over himself trying to apologize for the fact that he didn't know that I was the bride-to-be.

"It's fine, really," I insist but he pries the champagne glass out of my hand and replaces it with a pink Martini.

I chuckle knowing that this is something that his boss (or maybe my sister or my mom) insist that he do.

"I'm so sorry about the catering situation," my mom's friend rattles off.

She's tall, slim, and looks about twenty years younger than she really is after a lifetime of portion controlled food and daily workouts.

But she's also kind and more authentic than some of the other people that my mom hangs out with and I like her.

"It's okay," I say, nodding my head. "Actually, Lindsey and Mom took care of it so I don't really know what exactly happened."

"Okay, good. I just didn't want you to worry."

I give her half a smile and try to pull

myself away. I see my plan for the evening falling apart before my eyes.

I have arrived at the party with the intention of calling the whole thing off. I was supposed to first tell the valet and then the server and then maybe everyone else.

But if I can't even tell two people who couldn't care less that my engagement is off, how I am going to tell my relatives, my parents' friends, and God-forbid Alex's out of town guests.

But now seeing the sea of people and actually facing the idea of giving a speech or worse yet talking to each of the guests one-on-one, my body becomes rigid.

I freeze on the spot, unable to move.

"Shit, shit, shit," I mumble to myself.

Keeping my back to the room, I glide up the stairs, silently praying that no one sees me.

"Hey, you're here!" Lindsey yells at the top of the stairs.

Dressed in a tailored black dress that falls just below the knee and crosses in the back, my sister looks more like the bride-to-be than I do.

Her hair is cut short in a sleek bob and her face looks practically airbrushed.

She's wearing three-inch heels and walking perfectly in them regardless of her belly.

At six months pregnant, you can still barely see anything but a small protrusion on the outside of her dress.

Lindsey has always been tall, elegant, and thin. She has always known exactly how to style her clothes, how to do her hair, and how to apply her makeup.

In pictures, she always looks poised and beautiful, almost as if she had walked out of the society page of Coast.

She looks me up and down and shakes her head.

I glance at her, smiling at the corner of my lips. I know that she's judging me, but there's something else in her gaze.

"You can't wear that," she says, grabbing me by my elbow. "Mom is going to freak out."

She leads me to the master bedroom at the far end of the house. There are four other rooms attached to it; his and her bathrooms and his and her closets.

My mom's closet is about as big as my whole apartment. In addition to all of the built-ins, there is a large island with shelving and a runway-like area with a triple-fold mirror similar to the ones they have in bridal boutiques.

"You have to pick out something from her closet," Lindsey says.

I shake my head.

"You have to," Lindsey insists. "I think that the makeup and hair people haven't left yet so they can fix you up before you go down there and mingle with everybody."

"You know, I tried hard to look this good," I say, sitting down on the couch and looking at my reflection in the enormous standup mirror.

"Are you kidding me?" she asks. "No, you haven't. I have seen you try hard and this is not trying hard."

"Mom didn't tell you, did she?" I ask.

"Tell me what?" Lindsey asks, pulling out a light teal dress that's just loose-fitting enough to fit.

"The wedding is off."

"What are you talking about?" Lindsey whips her head around and stares at me.

"I can't believe that she didn't tell you."

I shake my head and pick at my cuticles.

"Tell me what? What's going on?" Her voice is desperate and out of control.

"I caught Alex cheating. Today. At lunch. With his boss."

"No," Lindsey hisses under her breath

"Yes, and apparently it's not a one-time thing."

"No…"

"She's married and they've been seeing each other since three years before he met me."

"So, he's been with her this whole time?" Lindsey asks, putting her hand over her mouth.

"Yep, five years. Apparently, he stopped seeing her for a year when we first met but then picked things up again."

"Holy shit," Lindsey whispers. "Why are you here? Why are we even having this party?"

"Good question," I say, raising my

eyebrows. "I told Mom and told her that I didn't want to go through with it anymore. I wanted to call it off and I don't want to have this stupid engagement party. She said that I can't unless I come here and tell everyone myself. In person."

8

EMMA

Lindsey puts her arm around my shoulders. I don't have anymore strength within me to hold it all back so tears start to flow.

"It's okay, it's okay," she repeats herself over and over again, but somehow her support makes it worse. Maybe *worse* is the wrong word. More painful.

We've never had much of a sisterly bond. We grew up together but we were never that close.

No matter what Lindsey says, I can't stop myself from crying and the tears continue to run down my face until my eyes are red, bloodshot, and completely puffy.

Suddenly, the closet door swings open and Mom comes in. Dressed in an impeccable Donna Karan suit, she looks like she could be one of the Real Housewives of Calabasas. Her hair is cut right below the ears and styled in such a way that not a single strand is out of place.

She's not surprised to see me even though I am surprised to see her.

"Alex and his family are waiting for you downstairs," Mom says nonchalantly.

It's almost as if she knew that we would both be here.

"She told you what happened, right?" Lindsey comes to my defense. "How could you make her go through with this?"

"Lindsey, you of all people should know that men are not perfect."

I glance over at my sister and peer into her eyes.

"What is she talking about?" I ask her quietly.

She ignores me, but tells Mom, "She cannot marry him if he's cheating on her."

"I'm not telling her to marry him. I'm telling her that we are *not* making a spectacle of this party. You and I have both worked really hard on it and we have people who have traveled from miles to get here. They stood in line at the airport. They got on airplanes. The least that we can do is to offer them some hors d'oeuvres, some nice music, dancing, and the view of the ocean. That's *the least* we can do."

I shake my head. She should be on my side, but of course she's not.

"In the meantime, you need to fix yourself up. You can't go to your engagement party looking like you just found out that your fiancé has been cheating on you."

I glance at my reflection in the mirror.

I look ragged and exhausted.

I look like I haven't slept in days.

"I'm going to buy you some time, but I expect you downstairs in half an hour looking like the most beautiful bride-to-be that anyone at this party has ever seen."

I nod my head slightly, not really agreeing, but not really fighting her either.

I'm here.

Alex is here.

My family is here.

His family is here.

Why not just get this awful night over with?

Twenty-five minutes later, I walk downstairs looking like someone I have never looked like before.

My face has been airbrushed with foundation along with some sort of sparkling powder that makes my cheekbones look like they have been elevated by two inches.

The makeup artist has even applied makeup to my chest and the curve near the top of my breasts to make them look bigger and rounder.

My hair has been straightened and styled to make it fall softly around my shoulders. I'm dressed in my mom's little black dress. It's one of her many and it's one of the bigger sizes that she owns.

Luckily, Lindsey found it in the back, otherwise I'd be stuck with some sort of loose-fitting floor-length number that she only wears to pool parties.

Despite all of this, when I first see Alex, I'm glad that she made me dress up.

He looks like a prince waiting for me at the bottom of the winding staircase. His hair is slicked back with just enough product to give it that extra shine without looking goopy and gross.

With the sunlight streaming in through the enormous floor-to-ceiling windows in the foyer, Alex's eyes sparkle and his skin gets a beautiful beige coloring to it.

This is what photographers call the golden hour of the day and the one that Mom has hired to document the evening snaps a million photos of me walking down the stairs toward my *beloved*.

There's another photographer positioned across from Alex to capture his reaction. I also spot a cameraman out of the corner of my eye right before Alex takes my hand and pulls me in close for a kiss.

I want to pull away, but the sound in the whole room dies down as everyone holds their breath watching us. Alex's lips feel soft and delicate on mine. Almost as if they are still begging for forgiveness.

Mine on the other hand are pursed and tense. I want to pull away and smack him across the face, but with everyone watching, I can't.

"Emma," Alex says, wrapping his arm tightly around my waist. "I'd like you to meet my Uncle Gil and Aunt Elaine."

The introductions to the family members begins. As soon as we make a little bit of small talk with one group of relatives, he quickly rushes me away to meet another and another. After I am introduced to every one of his parents' siblings, all of whom have decided to travel across the country to attend this engagement party, then we move on to his parents' friends.

My stomach rumbles and I use that as an excuse to take a break. There are servers circulating with hors d'oeuvres, but there's also a large hors d'oeuvre table at the far end of the sitting room.

The walls of my parents' home are linen white and the windows all overlook the deep blue ocean on the horizon. It's a beautiful day, without a cloud in the sky.

It takes all of my strength to not rush out of the French doors leading to the sparkling pool, run past the guest house, and throw myself over the cliff.

"Thank you for being here," Alex says, reaching for my waist.

I take two steps away from him and load my plate with some carbohydrates.

"I'm not here for you," I say blankly. "My mom refused to call off the party."

"I know. I asked her not to."

I stare at him.

Of course, he did and, of course, she went along with it.

"Don't be mad at her," Alex pleads. "I'm the asshole. It's just that my parents and all of our family and friends flew in and I didn't want to make everything that happened public until we were sure what was going to happen."

I start to laugh.

"What's so funny?"

"You really have a way with words. Everything that happened? I love how that statement assigns no fault. The only reason this wedding is off is because of *you*. I didn't do anything wrong."

"I know," he says, casting down his eyes.

"That's not what I meant. I just didn't want to…"

"What?" I press him.

"I am embarrassed, okay? I didn't want to tell my parents what I did. I didn't want all of my family and friends to know. I want to make things right with you. I want you back."

I shake my head and let out a long sigh.

"You were with Jen for three years before you met me," I whisper. "Then for two more years afterward."

"Just one more year," he corrects me and I tighten my grip on my Martini glass, stopping myself from throwing it at his head. "Look, I'm not proud of that, but you have to believe me. It was nothing. Jen and I just got into this habit of hanging out together at work. That's all that it was. Some people like to go to the same restaurant for lunch. Other people like to order the same things. We like to have a quickie in the office. It didn't mean anything, for her or for me. She had no plans to ever leave her husband and she never wanted to break up her family."

"What about you?" I ask. "I know all about her intentions, but what about yours?"

A few people approach the hors d'oeuvres table and it's no longer safe for us to talk here even in hushed tones.

Alex motions for me to follow him out back. At first, I hesitate, but then I see a large group of my dad's relatives heading in our direction and I quickly escape through the sliding glass door.

When my parents bought this house, it came with a big round pool and an attached hot tub. The view from the house is beautiful, but the pool was an older design with tile all around.

Last year, they had updated it by making it a modern rectangle to match the angular design of the rest of the house. They also resurfaced it with a pebble finish that gave it a more natural coloring.

"This view is magnificent," Alex remarks, looking out past the infinity edge and how it meets with the spaciousness of the Pacific Ocean below.

"Yes, it is," I agree.

I had reveled in this view every day for a

month when my parents were in Europe last summer. Just because I live in a crappy apartment and refuse their money, it doesn't mean that I don't appreciate the finer things in life.

"I want to buy a home here with you," Alex says.

"No," I say sternly.

"It doesn't have to be here. We can get something in Laguna Beach, overlooking the cliffs. We can get something in San Diego or Santa Barbara. Wherever you want."

"No," I repeat myself.

"It doesn't have to have a view of the ocean. We can have a view of the city. Imagine living in the Hollywood Hills with all of Los Angeles sparkling below you."

I turn around to face him.

The sun has dipped over the horizon a long time ago and the backyard's twinkling lights dance in his irises.

"You don't get it, do you? I *don't* want to live with you. I *don't* want to marry you. I *don't* want to be with you."

The words come from the pit of my

stomach, originating from some inner strength that I didn't realize that I had.

But when Alex turns his back to me and walks away, tears resurface and slide down my cheeks.

9

EMMA

A few minutes later, someone touches my shoulder. I whip my head around expecting to see Alex, but it's my mom. Somehow, that's worse.

"I can't do this," I say, shaking my head.

She brings her hands over to my face and wipes away my tears.

"Look up and blink. That will make them dry up."

"I can't stop thinking about this."

"That's the other secret to not crying," she jokes. "Not thinking about it."

"You have to tell people that the wedding is off."

"No," Mom says, shaking her head. "The night is almost done. Everyone is having a great time. Why ruin it?"

"This feels like a farce."

"It is a farce," she corrects me. "Since when has any party not been that? We are here to celebrate you and Alex. It doesn't matter if we're here to celebrate your engagement."

"What are you even talking about?" I ask, shaking my head.

"You don't have to be so dramatic, honey. You always take things so seriously. Everyone is here to have a good time. We all need a reason for a little party, especially at someone else's expense."

"So, what's going to happen… afterward?" I ask.

"You and Alex are going to figure things out. If for some reason you do agree to break up, then you can just call all of these guests or even email all of them and tell them that the wedding is off. No big deal. But if you don't want to wait and want to stop this party tonight, then the microphone is right there. You're welcome to go ahead and use it."

My mom narrows her eyes. She knows that she's asking me to do the impossible.

I have never been good at public speaking. For everyone else in my family, it seems to come as second nature. They can just take the microphone and make all sorts of statements that make everyone in the room feel good, whether or not they are true.

I can't do that.

I can't even make a basic speech in honor of someone let alone stand up there and tell 200 people why I'm no longer getting married.

Mom walks away and I follow her into the living room.

I take a deep breath. The band is about to start to play and this is the time to do a toast if a toast is going to be done. I know that my mom and my dad probably have something planned. I don't want to hear it.

Cold sweat runs down my spine and I'm thankful for the fact that I'm wearing a black dress that will hide whatever pit stains are inevitably going to appear underneath my arms.

I take a deep breath and take a few steps toward the microphone, but then someone stops me.

It's Alex.

He slips his arm under mine intertwining it just below the elbow.

He then pulls me close to him and whispers, "If you are planning on telling anyone that the engagement is off, then make sure that you remember that all of your parents' money is invested in our hedge fund."

I pull away from him, narrowing my eyes.

"Are you threatening me?" I gasp.

"No, of course not. I just want you to remember that our families are already interconnected and I wouldn't want anything bad to happen."

We both know that it's a threat and I have no idea how to respond to it. Before I can take a moment to decide, Alex grabs the microphone with one hand and pulls me closer with the other.

He clears his throat and calls for everyone to pay attention. When everyone's eyes are up front, the house lights dim and a spotlight focuses on us.

He opens his mouth and starts to tell the audience the story of how we met and what happened the first time he told me that he loved me. The speech is eloquent and punctuated with pauses for laughter and contemplation.

He doesn't make himself look like a saint, but he does make everyone in that room love him because of how much he loves me. Of course, he doesn't tell them about Jen or anything that happened today, but when it's over, I certainly can't.

People are tearing up at his words and his charm and even if I were to suddenly tell them every last dirty secret, I don't think that they would side with me.

The thing is that I don't need them to side with me. The decision is all mine.

I know this. Still, I can’t bring myself to tell everyone the truth.

Luckily, the rest of the speeches are much shorter and more concise. My mom only says a few words and she never says only a few words.

Lindsey passes altogether and Alex's parents just give us a brief congratulations. I don't know if they suspect, but I'm relieved that this part of the evening is over.

Finally, it is time for dessert and dancing.

When the music starts roaring, I step outside for some more fresh air. The area by the pool is crowded and I want some alone time so I go around the side of the house.

There's a secondary patio along with a smaller outdoor dining table and four chairs.

I collapse into one, pushing off my heels and propping up my sore feet on another.

I don't see that someone is sitting across from me until he clears his throat.

10

EMMA

"I didn't mean to scare you," he says after I jump.

"No, you didn't." It's a lie and we both know it, but he lets me off the hook.

Suddenly, I feel self-conscious. How could I have not seen him before?

"I can go if you need some time alone," he says in his smooth, velvety voice.

I hesitate and he leans over the picnic table, bringing his face out of the shadows.

His eyes are piercing and black. His hair is silky and dark, falling slightly into his face.

There is a mysterious aura to him, almost as if he doesn't quite belong here.

Then again, who does?

"No, you don't have to leave," I say. "I like the company."

I wait for him to ask me what's wrong, but he doesn't.

I appreciate that. We spend some time enjoying each other's presence without the need to fill the void with conversation.

"So, you're the bride-to-be, huh?"

I shrug and say, "I guess."

"Maybe not?" he asks, raising one eyebrow higher than the other.

"Absolutely not," I say.

This is the first time that I've ever told anyone at this party the truth, outside of my immediate family, and it feels incredibly liberating.

For the first time, I'm not pretending that I am someone that I'm not.

For the first time, I'm not covering up for some awful deed in order to save face.

By the way, why is it that I should feel humiliated by what Alex did?

I didn't do anything wrong.

He's the asshole.

What's wrong with exposing him for being this terrible person who would do something so evil to someone that he supposedly loves?

"I just found out that Alex isn't exactly who I thought he was," I say quietly, looking out into the distance. "I was going to break up with him. I did break up with him. Then my mom refused to call off this party and his parents and his family members already flew in so… Here we are."

"None of them know that you're not really getting married?"

I shake my head and say, "Besides my mom and sister, you're the only person at this party who knows the truth."

"Nice." He smiles.

"But I don't even know your name."

I laugh and he laughs along with me.

He's dressed in a black suit but without a tie and with an open collar. He looks both elegant and casual at the same time.

Unlike some of the people at the party, he doesn't look uncomfortable in his suit. In fact, it's quite the opposite.

He looks like he could sleep in it, attend a board meeting, and go surfing and somehow it would always be a fit.

"I'm Emma," I say, extending my hand. "Emma Scott."

"Nice to meet you, Emma," he says and I like the feel of my name in his mouth.

When our hands touch, a shock of electricity sends the hairs on the back of my arm straight into the air.

I laugh, but he just smiles at the corner of his mouth. His lips are small, but full.

There's a lusciousness to them that is difficult to ignore.

Yet his smile is crooked. It's not the same on both sides, giving him a kind of whimsical quality.

"I'm Liam," he says. "Liam Parish."

I smile to myself at the symmetry with which he speaks, mirroring my own.

I want to ask who invited him here, but I can't quite come up with the right wording to stop me from sounding rude.

"So, what do you do, Liam?"

"Lots of things and a little bit of everything."

I look up at him and our eyes meet. That question is supposed to be answered with a job title, but he challenges me and I like that.

"I like to surf. I like to ride horses. I like to hike and swim and read. How about you?"

I pause for a moment to think about it.

Those all sound like hobbies. I think to myself. I haven't had much time to spend on my hobbies in years.

"I'm a writer. Journalist. I work for Coast Magazine."

"Oh, I see. How do you likc it there?"

"It's interesting. I've always wanted to write for a living and I love that I can actually do that. Whether or not I make enough money to make a living, that's a whole other thing."

"Doesn't seem like that's something you have to worry about," Liam says, looking around the house and the grounds.

I clench my jaw to keep the anger at bay.

"For your information, I don't take any money from my parents whatsoever. They're rich, but I'm not. I make my own way in life."

Liam focuses his gaze on me, narrowing his eyes.

I expect him to apologize, but he doesn't.

Instead he just looks at me as if I am the one who has said something wrong.

"I didn't mean anything by that." He finally caves.

"Yeah, no one ever does."

"Is that something that's important to you?" he asks.

"What? Living on the money that I make and nothing else?"

He shrugs and says, "That's not usually how it's done in these parts."

"I don't need a lecture on how nepotistic and self-centered people in Los Angeles can be. Everyone seems to do just about anything for money and access, but I'm not like that."

I cross my arms and get up.

"I'm sorry," he says after a long pause.

"Doesn't matter. I'm having a bad day."

If we had met under normal circumstances, I would have never jumped down his throat like that. He didn't really say anything out of line and perhaps I was too quick to anger.

"So, what kind of stuff do you work on for Coast?" Liam asks. "I've seen it at

Barnes & Noble, but I've never picked it up."

"Too many pictures of the ocean?" I ask.

"Too many pictures of carefully curated dining room tables with their centerpieces of lemons and silverware."

I laugh.

I like his sense of humor. It's understated and surprising, something that I desperately need right now to take my mind off my life.

"We write a lot of articles about interior design especially for coastal houses, but mainly it's a lifestyle magazine with recipes and ideas for parties and that kind of thing. There are also a few spots for features. The one that I'm working on now seems kind of far-fetched and not a great fit for the magazine, but my boss has a stick up her ass about getting me to write it so I have to figure out how to do that."

"Oh, yeah?" he asks.

I nod.

I don't know why I feel the need to tell him all of this.

It's not really a need, but a desire to share.

A part of me suspects that it might have something to do with the fact that he's the first person who has actually showed any interest in my work and in me in a long time.

"Tell me about it," he says, shifting his weight forward and leaning closer to me.

"I pitched a story about a reclusive writer that no one knows anything about. It seemed like an impossible assignment at the time and is not a great fit for the magazine, but I had nothing else for the pitch meeting so I went with it. I had no idea that she would actually take me up on it."

"Who is the reclusive writer?"

"D. B. Carter. Ever heard of him?"

Liam shakes his head and says, "I'm not much of a reader."

"Well, a lot of people like him. He's an independently published author."

"Meaning?"

"He sells and publishes his books on Amazon and other platforms by himself."

"What's so special about him?" Liam asks.

"He sells a lot of books. He writes epic fantasy with some romance. He makes a lot of money. He has sold millions of copies. He has been on all the big lists like The New York Times and USA Today. You know what else?"

"What?"

"He publishes a book every month or so. He's dominating the space and no one knows one thing about him. Or even if he's a he at all."

"It might be a woman?" Liam asks.

"Pseudonyms are really popular so, technically, yes, D. B. Carter could be a man or woman. I'm just assuming that it's a man…unfortunately, being a white male is kind of a default setting."

"So, how are you going to go about finding him or her?"

"I have no idea. Do you know anything about searching for people on the Internet?"

"No, not really. I don't even have a social media account."

"Well, D. B. Carter does. Actually, he is quite active, but he never posts any pictures or personal information of any kind. Just promos for the books."

"Can you just reach out to the account and ask for an interview?"

"Yeah, I guess. That's probably what I'm going to have to do."

"Huh," Liam says, leaning back against the picnic table. "Have you ever thought it was more than one person?"

"What do you mean?"

"Well, you said that the author is really prolific. They publish a bunch of books. Maybe it's not just one person doing the work. Maybe there's a bunch of ghostwriters."

"I thought about that, but the work is too consistent and too good. If anything, it could be a few authors working together under one pen name. That's basically the mystery that Coast wants me to uncover. Exactly how I do that with a person who doesn't reveal anything personal anywhere on the Internet I have no idea."

There's a long pause and it hangs in the air between us like a cumulus cloud. I realize that Liam might be onto something. Sometimes the people that know nothing at all can present a perspective that's impossible to see from up close.

It never occurred to me that D. B. Carter could be two writers. There are numerous examples of this in the romance genre. Kennedy Fox, for one. They are two writers who alternate writing different chapters of the same book and then do the promotions together.

Could D. B. Carter be someone like that?

Could D. B. Carter be two women like that?

Liam and I sit together for a long time until I start to shiver.

This city is a desert with little humidity. Once the sun goes down, the earth turns cold, and your mother's little dress becomes insufficient.

"I'm going inside," I tell Liam. "See you there?"

He gives me a nod and a faraway smile that assures me that I won't see him again.

11

LIAM

I don't belong here.

I haven't been in LA in close to two years and now I remember why.

Plastic faces.

Plastic personalities.

Plastic lifestyles.

Everyone here is obsessed with money.

It's unfair to put everyone into the same pot and it's even more unfair to use the guests of this party as a representation for all of Los Angeles, but I can't help myself.

I ran into Alex by accident. I knew him back in middle school. We were friends but after my family moved away, we lost touch.

I shouldn't be here, but I couldn't say no.

There's no one around and I love it that way. I'm not much of a people person. It's too crowded inside and the views from up here are breathtaking.

The breeze picks up and I close my eyes and enjoy the way it caresses my face. It's both refreshing and freeing.

I can almost taste the salt in the air. It feels so good against my skin that I actually wonder if I should maybe move back here. Not to the city and not in a development, but maybe get a little spread of a few acres on a cliff somewhere overlooking the vastness of the Pacific.

That's the main reason why I am here. I know that Alex's hedge fund is doing quite well. As soon as I had mentioned that I have some money of my own, he started calling me about coming in for an investment meeting.

A woman sits at the picnic table right next to me without seeing me. She's so buried in her grief and consumed by her sadness that she practically looks straight through me.

I don't recognize her at first, but then she

starts talking and I remember where I know her from. She descended down the marble staircase like a princess. I wonder if I'm the only person at this party who knows that her fiancé waiting for her at the bottom doesn't deserve her.

Alex has a lot of positive attributes, but none of them are ones that will make him a good husband. He's bored easily, especially by women. And he's someone who needs to be entertained.

This woman sitting in front of me doesn't look like someone who is looking to put on a show. I don't mean that in an offensive way. It's just an observation.

Instead, she looks like someone who wants an equal partner.

Someone to love her, someone to be there for her, and someone to not cheat on her.

I'm the first guest that Emma tells that her engagement is off. I'm not so sure that this is actually the case because Alex does have a way with words and a way of getting what he wants, but I want to believe her.

She seems certain. She doesn't go into

any of the details, but she doesn't need to. I only knew Alex as a kid but I've seen him on social media years ago. He has always loved women. Many women.

After Emma leaves, I continue to sit at the picnic table staring at the dark ocean below. I give myself a few more minutes before I get up and go back inside.

"Liam! There you are!" Alex waves to me from across the room.

I see him trapped in a conversation with four older gentlemen who look like they play a lot of golf and I'm happy to come to his rescue.

"He's one of my oldest friends. I've known this guy since middle school," Alex says.

After we all shake hands, the guy in the round spectacles asks, "What do you do for a living?"

"Bit of everything," I say, putting my weight on my back foot. "Now? A lot of woodworking."

Silence falls between us.

Alex smiles at the corner of his mouth,

amused by my approach to this very normal line of questioning.

I don't know if it's just a man thing or if women do this as well, but I've noticed that whenever I'm in a group of strangers we all seem to measure each other up by figuring out where we stand in the financial pecking order.

"Actually, Liam is here to talk to me about getting some of his money invested in the fund," Alex cuts me off just as I'm about to open my mouth and say some more inappropriate things. "Liam, George here is one of my biggest investors."

"Oh, yeah? What are your thoughts?"

I look up at a man with reddish blond hair and freckles, which gives him a boyish look.

"I wouldn't trust my money with anyone else," George says. "Although from what I've heard, he's not taking on any new people."

"Where did you hear that?" Alex asks, taking a sip of scotch.

"Your father. I had a few friends that I thought would place their money with you as well, but when you were busy, your secretary put them through to your father and that's what he told me."

"Yeah, we've had a few conversations about that. He wants to limit the number of investors that we bring in and increase the amount of money that they give to us. I think that there's nothing wrong with opening ourselves up to more money from friends and family. Please don't worry about that. One of these days, Father will let me run this thing the way that it should be run and everything will be fine."

After George and his friends walk away to mingle with the rest of the crowd, Alex turns to me and laughs.

"I forgot how much you like to fuck with people," he says.

"Why?" I ask innocently. "Did I offend him?"

Alex shakes his head and gets us another round of drinks.

"I just happen to think that there's more to us than what they have in the bank," I say. "I'm sorry that George didn't agree with me."

"That is something George will never agree with."

Alex uses this as a lead way to start telling me about his investment fund. I know that it's probably a good idea to put my money in there, he has an excellent reputation and that's technically why I came here, but I'm not really in the mood to talk about it now.

I glance over to Emma, who is standing against the wall, practically hugging it.

"I completely forgot." Alex is ushering me toward her. "Let me introduce you to my fiancée."

I hesitate but I have no choice. I decide to take her lead. If she pretends that we have never met, then I'll go along with it.

Alex introduces her by grabbing her left hand and showing me her big ring. From the outside, you wouldn't know that anything is wrong.

I guess that's the thing about pretending. We all do it, right?

That's what everyone keeps telling me and that's exactly why I live out there on my acreage all by myself as far away from people as possible.

After we shake hands, Emma cowers into herself but remains standing before me. In the bright light of the room, she looks small and insecure, but still undeniably beautiful. She has big eyes and beautiful shiny hair that cascades down her shoulders.

Alex keeps talking even though neither of us give him much encouragement except for a brief nod here and there. Instead, our eyes stay focused on one another's and I realize just how difficult this moment is for her.

"Emma and I are planning on going to Laguna Beach this weekend. We got a suite right on the beach. It's not going to be particularly warm. It's not Hawaii, of course, or the Caribbean, but you know, we'll try to have fun."

Emma's eyes dart to Alex.

She shakes her head, but just a little bit. I wait for her to finally cave and forgive him, but she surprises me.

"No," she says.

The word comes out strong and categorical.

Assertive.

"What?" Alex asks.

A plastic smile appears on his face, the kind that we all use when we want to get someone to stop saying things that we don't agree with.

"No, I'm not going to Laguna Beach this weekend and no, Liam, Alex is *not* my fiancé."

"Honey, let's just not do this right here."

"Okay," she says, crossing her arms. "Let's not. The only problem is that this is our engagement party. This is my parents' home and you're here. *Why* are you here?"

"You know perfectly well," he says under his breath. "My family and their friends flew in from New York and everywhere else. I couldn't just *not* come."

"You could have *not* been fucking your boss and then we wouldn't be in this mess."

I take a step back and my mouth opens a little bit. I have never seen a scene like this unfold in front of my eyes.

Of course, we have seen plenty of this

on television and movies, but to actually witness the unraveling of an engagement, that's quite something.

"Look what we are doing," Alex says. "You're making my friend uncomfortable."

I raise my hands up in the air and say, "No."

"Listen," Emma says, quieting her voice. "I told you that this wedding is off. Yet you can't seem to get that through your head. I know that it is one thing for my mom to say stuff like that, but *you* are the one that hurt me. You are the one that I caught cheating. It's over. You clearly never cared about me and you clearly don't now. Why are you here putting on this charade?"

12

EMMA

I don't know why I am here.

I don't know why I'm talking to him.

I feel like Liam and I shared a moment and I thought that I might have found a friend. Maybe not a friend, but at least a friendly face. But looking at him now, I know he's on Alex's side.

I don't care. I deserve better than this asshole and I know that even if no one else does.

Alex keeps trying to talk to me, but I just walk away. I've repeated myself enough and it's still not getting through to him.

Alex follows me until I disappear in the bathroom.

Frustrated, annoyed, and trapped in my own parents' home, I open my phone and stare at the messages. I scroll through a million useless tweets and pretty images on Instagram.

A few videos pop up, but I quickly turn those off. I don't have the energy to watch or engage on any level beyond the very basic.

I'm not sure what leads me to *his* social media besides my own frustration at my predicament, but I search for D. B. Carter's name in the search bar on Facebook. He has over 100,000 followers, which is quite a lot for a fantasy author without a television show or who isn't JRR Martin or Tolkien.

I scroll through the main posts on his page trying to glean any personal information, but there are just posts about his new releases and promotions. There's a free book and there is another book on sale for $.99. Along with that, he also has a brand-new release that just came out last week.

I turn my attention to Amazon and decide to count up all the books he has written. I get to seventy-eight before I lose track when my sister knocks on the door.

Brooke is two years younger than I am and she is as girlie as Lindsey. Brooke is something of a mystery to both Lindsey and me. She's a big girl, like I am, but unlike me she actually seems to have mastered this whole-body acceptance thing and loves herself for who she is.

She likes fashion, makeup, and dressing up. She has an Instagram with about 50,000 followers and she posts new pictures every day with an outfit of the day. She's not a huge influencer, but whatever she promotes, people buy and a lot of brands know that.

"Listen, can you please stop moping about your engagement? Come out here and look at this bikini picture that I'm about to post."

I open the door and reluctantly let her in.

The picture is of her sitting on one of the loungers in front of the pool, earlier in the day. She's lying on her side and has an inquisitive and flirty expression on her face.

Brooke is plus-sized. I'm not exactly sure what size she wears now, but she's a good twenty pounds heavier than I am.

"Are you showing me this to make me feel bad?" I ask, looking at how she spreads herself out in the picture.

"Feel bad? Why?"

"You look fucking hot." She's so full of confidence, it just makes me want to cry. Not only did I just get cheated on, but I will also probably never look as beautiful as she does in that picture.

"You're just saying that," she says, rolling her eyes and shrugging her shoulders.

Dressed in a yellow floral print dress that accentuates all of her ample assets, she looks like a goddess. Lindsey is pretty, tall, thin, and everything that the media will tell you an attractive girl is supposed to look like, but it's Brooke who is drop dead gorgeous.

"I told you," Brooke says. "You can't listen to Mom. Lindsey means well, but she's clueless. They both have no idea what kind of world we are living in."

"Excuse me?" Mom walks up to us and clears her throat. "Are you actually advising my child not to listen to me?"

She likes to say that kind of thing to get under our skin and it works every time.

Mom glances at Brooke's phone. Brooke clicks through some of the photos, stopping on the last one where she is lying on her back with her legs spread out. She shows it to Mom, specifically to gauge her level of shock. If she isn't appalled enough, then there's no way that she will be posting it.

Mom doesn't take the bait and instead says, "Honey, you know that I think that you are beautiful, right? No matter what you're wearing or how you are putting yourself out there."

Then to put the nail in the coffin, she goes over and presses her lips to Brooke's forehead for a kiss.

Brooke looks angry, but I wait.

If Mom adds a "but" or any other kind of qualifier to that statement then Mom remains the judgmental, old-fashioned, and out of touch person that we both know that she is. But if she leaves it at that…then Mom wins.

"Okay, I will leave you two alone. I know that you have a lot to talk about," Mom says and my mouth drops open.

Brooke is fuming, but her anger is just below the surface. She runs a website promoting body acceptance for women of all sizes. But what strangers don't know is that she also does it to get a rise out of Mom.

"Wow, is this how it's going to be? Does Mom finally get it after all this time?" she asks when Mom gets out of earshot.

"You know, honey," Mom says, tucking her head back into the room. "In my day, women tried to find the most flattering clothes they could because we all knew we had our imperfections, no matter our size."

There.

It happened.

It finally *fucking* happened.

Mom hasn't changed at all. She just learned how to bite her tongue and stay in her lane.

I work my eyes over to Brooke, who

unlike me, has never been particularly shy in keeping her mouth shut.

I admire her greatly for that, something that I rarely say out loud.

In fact, it's something that I have never told her.

"There are no such things as flattering or unflattering clothes," Brooke says, crossing her arms. "There are clothes that I want to wear and there are clothes that I don't want to wear. I'm choosing to embrace all parts of me and love me for who I am. I'm not going to spend my days hating myself and killing myself with diet pills."

My mom is about to say something else when Brooke cuts her off again.

"In my day, Mom, women realize that all bodies are beautiful and that we can wear whatever the hell we want."

With that, Brooke drops the metaphorical mic and walks out of the bathroom, shutting the door in Mom's face.

I realize in this moment that I have never admired my sister more. She has always been the one to speak her mind and to challenge authority, but this is exactly the kind of courage that I needed to see today.

Mom wants me to be quiet.

She wants me to forgive Alex because men make mistakes or whatever the hell she said.

I don't have to accept someone treating me like shit as the status quo. I deserve better and I can demand better.

"Wow," I say, taking Brooke by the arm and leading her out to the balcony on the opposite side from the party.

"I loved the expression on her face when she saw the last picture." Brooke laughs.

"You know that despite all of that she loves you, right?" I ask.

Brooke shakes her head.

"No?" I ask.

"She sees us, her children, as a reflection of her. I don't think she really sees us as independent people. Lindsey looks and lives her life according to the rules. She's tall and beautiful and she takes care of herself. She has a wealthy husband and a big house. I'm not Lindsey."

"I don't think that she wants you to be Lindsey. She loves you for you."

"No," Brooke says. "She doesn't even know who I am. I doubt that she has ever even been on my website. She has no idea what I stand for. She has no idea what all of those videos I make mean. I know that she won't say it out loud, but she thinks that fat people are bad people. She thinks that there's something wrong with them and their will or their way of life that makes them that way."

I shrug.

I don't really know how to respond. That's pretty much what my mom thinks.

"Why are you taking her side anyway? She's the one that made you go through with this party. She's the one that still thinks that you should marry that asshole."

"She told me that men make mistakes and that we have to be accommodating," I say. "She told me that Dad cheated on her before they got married."

Brooke stares at me. I don't know if she knows this and I debated with myself as to whether or not I should tell her.

But then she rolls her eyes and leans over the balcony with exasperation.

"Dad has been cheating on her their whole life. If she thinks that it only happened before they were married, then she is delusional."

My mouth drops open.

"What are you talking about?" I ask.

13

EMMA

I stare at my sister. She is someone that I have admired my whole life even though she's younger than I am. She's always had the kind of confidence that I craved, but I know that confidence never came that easily to her.

In college she was actually quite shy. She never felt like she was good enough and she was always on a diet. Then something happened. She started posting all of these very empowering messages on social media and even got herself branded as something of an influencer.

Now, with that one statement, something changes.

It's almost as if the person that I thought I knew has disappeared.

I shake my head and ask, "What are you talking about?"

She turns away from me and starts to walk away, but I grab her arm.

"Tell me," I demand to know. "What do you know about Mom and Dad?"

She doesn't reply.

"How long have you known?"

She shakes her head.

"Why are you telling me about this *now*?"

Her face falls. She wasn't supposed to tell me this and now she can't take it back.

"I wasn't going to say anything. I had no idea that she told you about his earlier infidelity. I've known about it for a while. I actually walked in on them."

"Walked in on who?"

"I was there when Mom caught Dad with his girlfriend. It was so embarrassing and I just wanted the earth to split open and swallow me whole."

My head starts to buzz.

I'm immediately transported to earlier

today when I walked in on them. Anger starts to boil inside of me.

My mom had gone through the exact same thing and yet she stood there and told me to take my fiancé back.

What the hell is wrong with her?

"Tell me exactly what happened," I demand to know.

She takes a deep breath.

"We were out at a restaurant for dinner. Just the two of us. This is after you went to college and I was the only one who was left living at home."

"Uh-huh." I nod.

"We decided to stop by Dad's office and drop off some food. It was actually my idea. Mom didn't want to go. I wonder if she had her suspicions."

She stops talking and looks down at the floor.

"What happened next?" I nudge her.

"The lights were still brightly lit everywhere except for in his office. No one was around except for a few associates here and there working in their cubicles. Mom knocked and when he didn't answer, she tried to walk away. I heard some commotion in there. I opened the door and that's when I saw them. Him and some girl. She looked at least twenty years younger. How pathetic, right?"

I shrug.

I don't know what to say.

She's right. It is pathetic.

But what do you do when it's your own father?

"What happened after that?" I ask.

"I ran away. Mom stayed behind, somewhat. The elevator was taking too long so I ran to the staircase and started sobbing on the landing."

I stared at a space somewhat behind her.

I want to ask what happened after that, but I already know.

If it happened when Brooke was still in high school, then Mom took him back.

"She promised that they were going to go to therapy," Brooke says. "I don't know if they ever did. When I tried to ask her about it again, she told me never to bring it up."

"Why didn't you tell me? Lindsey?"

"She was mortified. She begged me not to. I was also embarrassed. I didn't want you to think worse of Dad."

Mom did everything in her power to cover his tracks.

"That's the whole problem," I say after a long pause. "She protects him so much that she makes him into some sort of saint."

"You know, this is why I didn't want to tell you," Brooke says. "You take such hard lines. People are much more complicated than this. They make mistakes."

"What are you trying to tell me, Brooke?" I glare at her.

Narrowing my eyes, I purse my lips.

"Nothing," she says quickly.

"No, really. Is this your way of advising me to stay with Alex?"

"What you do with Alex is up to you," she says, shaking her head.

"Yes, I know that. Thank you but I don't need your permission to break up with or marry anyone," I say sarcastically.

Despite all of my admiration for her confidence and all of her bravery, it dawns on me that she's just a child. She has never had a serious relationship and she has no idea what it's like to be in one. Maybe that's why it’s so much easier for her to forgive Dad. Maybe that's why it's so much easier for her to think about forgiving Alex.

After all of this the last thing that I want to do is go back to the party. I spent most of the evening pretending that I'm still getting married and I have no intentions of continuing this farce.

Instead, I ask her if she wants something real to eat.

She laughs and we head to the kitchen.

The caterers and the chef are still there, cleaning up. There’s a large four tier cake sitting in the middle of the marble kitchen island. It makes me nauseous to even look at it, even though I know that it will be delicious.

I open the refrigerator and grab the first thing I see: a bag of fresh red cherries. Large and plump, they sparkle under the beautiful kitchen chandelier that my mom installed ahead of the party.

Brooke pulls out a can of whipped

cream, but after checking the ingredients, she puts it back and grabs the vegan kind.

We use the back staircase to head to Brooke's old room. It looks exactly like it did when she was in high school. There are posters draped in twinkle lights all over the walls.

There's a large stand-up mirror right across from her bed. It's hard to believe that a girl as young as ten had been sleeping in a king-size bed all of her life when most kids are happy with just a twin.

I pop a cherry into my mouth. I bite into it carefully to avoid the pit and then savor the explosion of sweetness that colonizes my mouth.

"These are probably some of the best cherries I've ever had," Brooke announces.

I laugh because she says that often. Cherries are her favorite and that's why Mom always keeps them stocked in the fridge, paying more than eight dollars a bag at Whole Foods without even blinking an eye.

"Did I tell you about my new assignment at work?" I ask.

14

EMMA

"I'm going to have to write a story on D. B. Carter," I say and wait for her reaction.

It was actually she who first brought it up and suggested that I investigate him. She likes to read a lot of urban fantasy and fantasy romances and D. B. Carter is one of the biggest names out there among the indie authors.

"You did not!" Brooke squeals. "Seriously?"

"Yes. I pitched it when I had no other ideas and Corrin thought it was a great one and, of course, took it on. This is all your fault!"

"No, no, no. This is going to be so fun." She laughs. "You know that you're going to solve one of the biggest literary mysteries out there."

"Are there a lot of literary mysteries?" I ask, tilting my head. "I mean, come on."

"Okay, maybe not, but don't be so negative."

"How could I not be? I have to do all of this research on a person who does not want to be found and I have to turn it in by Monday. What do I even do *if* I find out who he is? It's not like he's going to let me interview him."

"Okay, it's probably not a *he* so you have to stop saying that," she says, emphasizing the word *he* dramatically.

I shrug.

"Come on," Brooke says. "I'm serious. Most people who write in that genre are women so there's a strong probability that this writer is a woman."

"Why does that matter?"

"She may be more open to talking to you after you find her."

"I kinda doubt that." I let out a deep sigh and roll my eyes. "Most indie authors promote themselves online and on social media. Why not? They want to sell their books. So, if I thought this person is obfuscating and hiding their identity on purpose, that means something. That means even if I go through all the trouble of finding out the truth, then it's all going to be for nothing. They're not going to give me an interview. They won't want to talk to me."

I'm exhausted and spent. The more I think about this, the less certain I am that I'm going to write this story at all.

"Okay," Brooke says, sitting on her bed and leaning toward me. "I'm going to help you."

"How?" I ask, throwing my hands up.

"I'll help you with everything, whatever you need. I'll help you do research. Besides, it's not like you're going to Laguna Beach to celebrate your engagement. You have three solid days to find something and I'm sure that's more than enough. You should come over and we can work on it together."

. . .

A LIGHT KNOCK on the door startles me at first, but it's just Lindsey.

"Mom said to find you because they're going to be cutting the cake," Lindsey says.

I shake my head. I thought that this horrible night would be over but I had completely forgotten about the cake.

"Listen, it's not going to be a big deal. You just stand there with Alex. He can say a few words and then you cut the cake. That's it."

She's saying this to be nice, but in reality, we both know there's a lot more to this.

On my way downstairs, Brooke squeezes my hand in solidarity. I glance over at Lindsey who gives me a sympathetic shrug.

Everyone feels bad for me but everyone also understands why I have to go through with this.

Everyone except for me.

Why am I going through with this?

When we get to the kitchen, I see Alex standing right next to the cake waiting for me like a real groom.

He walks over and gives me a small hug.

Somehow, it's almost as if nothing that happened today has registered with him at all. As long as we're going through the motions of the engagement party, he seems to think that we are still engaged.

He takes my hand and walks me through the double doors into the living room where everyone is waiting. We approach the DJ who has just introduced us as the future Mr. and Mrs. Wetterling and Alex confidently takes the mic.

This is the part that I hate; speeches.

I hate giving speeches and I equally hate receiving them. I don't like when people say nice things in my honor. I've always felt like that ever since I was a little kid. It's hard to explain exactly what makes this practice so terrible except that there seems to be some sort of inauthenticity to it.

I mean, why make speeches about people when you both already know each other and everything about each other?

When my dad takes the microphone, he starts to tell the crowd all about the kind of girl that I used to be when I was little. He tells about how proud he is of me, but throughout this whole presentation, I feel like it's a lie.

If these people really knew me, then there would be no reason for the speech. Since they don't, then what's the point? My dad has always been good at speeches. He's not so good with the one-on-one, but he knows how to woo a crowd and how to make people laugh.

It's a skill that I lack, but luckily the fact that I'm a woman lets me off the hook for the most part.

My dad's speech is followed by Alex's dad's speech, which is similarly distant yet fun and inviting. His dad has years of experience buttering up investors and proves to be almost as charming as mine.

The words that our fathers say are powerful and kind and yet they make me feel like such a fraud. I know that they probably don't mean the things that they say, but I believe them anyway and it makes me feel like I'm the one who is lying to all of our guests.

When Alex's dad stops talking and hangs up the mic, I finally let out a sigh of relief. I take a sip of champagne and raise it a bit higher as a final acknowledgement of this engagement. I've had enough and I can't wait to go home in my own car.

But Alex stops me. He clears his throat, raises his glass, and asks for a few minutes of everyone's time.

"I just want everyone here to know," he begins, "that I don't deserve this woman who is standing by my side. I never did and I hope that I can go through my life making choices that will finally lead me to her.

"I have made a lot of mistakes, most of which I will hopefully take to the grave, but she is well aware of them and she has found it in her soul to forgive me. I never expected that and she deserves a lot better than me, but I appreciate it.

"I just want to tell you in front of all of these people that I love you more than you will ever know. Thank you so much for giving me a second chance, and then a third chance and then a fourth chance.

"Mainly, I just want to say thank you for forgiving my flaws and my mistakes. Thank you for sticking by me no matter what. I will spend the rest of my days trying to be the husband that you deserve."

The room explodes in applause and I freeze unable to move. I don't know what to say or do.

I just glare at Alex and hate him with all of my might.

How dare he say this to me?

How dare he dance around something that is so personal and intimate?

How dare he tell all these people half a truth and then leave me hanging to answer for the rest?

I swallow hard and the crowd cheers louder and louder. Then suddenly, they calm down and expect me to say something in return.

This is my chance.

This is my opportunity to tell everyone that the wedding is off because my fiancé has cheated on me with his boss.

I take the microphone and clear my

throat. I can count the number of speeches that I have made on one hand and most of those were work requirements and debate class.

My whole body starts to shake.

My mouth runs dry.

I take another sip of my champagne, but the tanginess makes my taste buds dry up.

"The ball is in your court," Alex whispers under his breath, just loud enough for me to hear.

I look out into the audience.

My eyes scan over my mom, my dad, Lindsey, and Brooke. My aunts and uncles are here and then somewhere in the middle of the group, I see *him*.

It's Liam. He's standing there and there is space all around him. Suddenly everyone else in the room disappears and it's just him and me.

He's one of the few people here who know the truth.

I look at him for guidance, pleading with my eyes.

What should I do?

What should I say?

He gives me a slight nod. It's followed by a smile. Suddenly, my chest tightens as I open my mouth.

“Thank you all for being here,” I say and the microphone makes a grotesque sound that sends shivers down my spine. “Thank you all for traveling such great distances and taking time out of your day and out of your life to celebrate us.”

I keep my voice low and the mic a little too far. When I bring it a little bit closer, it echoes again, overwhelming me. “I really appreciate seeing you all and the effort that you put into coming here to celebrate us.”

I realize that I'm repeating myself, but I need to gather the strength. My eyes focus on Liam again and suddenly I start to feel better.

He gives me a nod of support and I let out a sigh of relief. It washes over me like a wave, wrapping me in a cocoon of comfort.

“The thing is that despite how much I wish I could be a part of your family and that we could join our families together, I can’t do that at this point. Alex did something terrible. I just found out earlier today and the wedding is off. We're not engaged and we are not getting married. Please enjoy the party and the cake. My mom and sister have worked really hard to organize everything."

15

LIAM

I watch her walk over to the mic with Alex holding her hand, waiting to see what's going to happen. The girl that I met out back was broken and disappointed.

That's exactly the woman who I see before me in the front of the room. You don't have to be a psychologist to figure out that she's not very comfortable with getting praise or having nice things said about her.

She stands with her shoulders slumped down cowering behind the man who I'd heard hurt her to her very core.

After Alex's father speaks, telling stories about a child who doesn't seem at all like the kid that I remember, Alex takes the mic. I expect him to say something as flat and insincere as his father, but he doesn't. He uses the time to give her a failed apology.

Perhaps she had made it clear to him that they will not be getting married and he's just trying to do one last thing to convince her to stay.

I wonder if it will work.

Suddenly, the mousy, timid woman who was standing next to her fiancé comes alive. She takes the microphone, clears her throat into it, and tells him to fuck himself.

Everyone else in the room is shocked, but I tilt my head back and laugh with my whole body.

Then I clap.

Finally, Emma has done what is right by her.

Alex is an asshole. We all know that. The only way he and men like him will start acting the right way is if the women in their lives demand it.

Instead of covering up for him and being embarrassed over her supposed humiliation, Emma takes the microphone and tells everyone in the room that the wedding is off.

A few minutes later, I find her at the bar.

Everyone else is avoiding her, trying to pretend that she's invisible. The couple next to Emma even have their backs turned, probably hoping that she doesn't talk to them. It's not like they're not curious. But they'd rather just gossip among themselves.

I don't have the same problem.

"To think," I say, walking up to Emma. "To think that I was going to miss this engagement party. I would have never forgiven myself."

I extend my hand and she shakes it, looking at the bottom of her cocktail.

"You were… Marvelous." I look down and realize that we are still shaking hands. She pulls hers away and laughs uncomfortably.

"Listen, I know that was hard but that was the right thing to do."

"Yeah," Emma says, looking around the room. "It certainly doesn't feel like it. You're the only one here congratulating me."

"Doesn't matter," I say, shaking my head. "They can all go fuck themselves."

An older woman standing next to me

glares at us and I shrug my shoulders, refusing to apologize.

"What Alex did was terrible and he deserved to be called out," I say. "They forced you to have this engagement party."

I glance over at her and see her staring at her sisters and her mom near the kitchen.

"Yeah, it was the right thing to do, but then why do I feel like such an asshole?"

"Maybe that's how you know it's the right thing to do," I say.

We stand here for a few moments and when I get up to walk away, she stops me.

"Don't leave," Emma whispers. "I have a feeling that no one's going to talk to me if you do."

"Do you want them to?" I ask.

"No, I don't, but the fact that *they* don't want to makes it that much more awkward."

I give her nod a and stand by her side for a few moments.

"Hey, smooth move." A woman who looks a lot like Emma walks up to us. Emma introduces her as her younger sister Brooke and she gives me a cute smile.

"Want me to simply say that? I thought you were just going to play along."

"I get tired of playing along. I didn't want to be like Mom. I don't want to be covering for my husband in front of my grown children years from now. To *not* do that, I figured I might as well come out here and tell everyone the whole ugly truth."

"Well, I'm really proud of how brave you are," Brooke says after a pause. "Wasn't she brave?"

"I've never seen anyone be braver," I agree.

Brooke and I exchange looks and then look back at Emma who suddenly seems as lost as ever.

In movies, the camera never follows you to what happens after the main character makes a big speech on stage. There are all these moments of levity and exhilaration, but right after that they are quickly followed by deep valleys of despair.

That's exactly what Emma is going through now. I wish I knew her better to put my arm around her and for it to not be weird.

I'm glad that Brooke does it for me.

We stand together for a few minutes until Emma sees her dad who waves her over. She glances over at Brooke and begs her to come, but Brooke just shrugs her shoulders and tells her to go talk to him.

"What do you think your dad is going to say?" I ask.

"I have no idea. Probably nothing good," Brooke responds.

"He would want her to marry him anyway?"

"No. I meant he won't say anything good about Alex. I don't think he really wanted her to marry Alex in the first place. Alex has a certain reputation, in case you didn't know."

"I've heard a thing or two. I thought that he got over it and maybe found the one who would keep him from straying, but I guess not."

"I don't think there is one," Brooke says, shaking her head. "I think that certain people either cheat or they don't cheat. It has nothing to do with the person they're with. If Alex were someone with integrity, then he wouldn't cheat on anyone, regardless of what he thought about her. He would break up with her first if he were interested in someone else."

I look at her and her words take me back a little bit. She looks young, a little bit younger than Emma, but she is clearly wise beyond her years.

Brooke's also beautiful. Some guys would probably not be able to look past her weight, but it looks to me like it's nothing but an asset to her.

Brooke carries it well. Standing next to me, her shoulders are spread wide and her bosom is elevated. There's a confidence to her that's quite disarming and attractive.

I can't help but wonder what she's like on a date.

"I'm sorry that he hurt your sister," I say after a long pause. "She deserves a lot better and I told her that."

"There's no need to apologize. You are not the one that hurt her," Brooke says nonchalantly.

"Yeah, I guess not," I say.

16

EMMA

I want Brooke to come with me, but she refuses.

I know that it's probably best that I talk to Dad by myself, but I'm still afraid.

Even after all these years, I still feel like I'm his little girl and I don't want to disappoint him.

It's too late for that though.

As soon as my dad sees me, he turns on his heel and walks toward the bar. I catch up with him anyway.

"Okay," he says, waving to me with a glass of oak colored liquid in his right hand.

I'm not much of a drinker, but I decide that I need a little bit more liquid courage coursing through my veins to get through this conversation.

My father is in his early 60s and is only now getting a little bit of salt in his hair.

He likes to work out and stay in shape. His skin has a nice tan to it, appropriate for someone who spends a lot of time on the tennis court.

He tried to encourage all three of his daughters to take up tennis, but only Lindsey answered the call. Still, that didn't stop him from sending us to tennis camp and getting us private tutors.

For the longest time, he seemed to believe that if only Brooke and I had the right instructor then we would fall in love with the sport that he loves. That hasn't happened.

On the weekends, Dad likes to play golf.

While I have enjoyed it the few times that I have played, that's not an activity that women are typically encouraged to play, especially not in his circle.

The golf course seems to be the domain for the partners and the few occasional associates, which almost all of them are men.

I know that the firm now employs a number of female associates and even has a few partners, but I'm not sure whether they are laying out the red carpet for them to spend their weekends with everyone else at the club.

"So, the wedding is off?" Dad asks, taking a seat behind the bar.

There are a few people his age milling around him but they quickly scatter as soon as he sits down and invites me to take the seat next to him.

"You know them?" I ask.

"They work for me," he says nonchalantly.

Despite the fact that he's an attorney, he is an expert at the understatement.

The culture of our world seems to be going in the direction of exuberance and exaggeration with words like *awesome* and *great* being thrown around all over the place, but my dad doesn't play that game.

If he were to say that he *knows* someone

then they are likely friends, but not very close ones.

If he were to *call* someone a friend…

Well, frankly, I don't think that he has ever bestowed that word on anyone besides our dog.

Dad turns his chair toward me and props up his head.

Suddenly, he looks exhausted.

It's not just because he is head deep into a very difficult and high-profile trial, this has to do with me.

"I'm sorry. I should've told you sooner, but I actually thought that maybe Mom did."

"I thought that after all these years you would know that your mother and I aren't on the closest terms."

He laughs, tossing his head back and shaking it slightly from side to side.

"I thought that maybe you two talked about things that involve us kids."

He furrows his eyebrows and moves a little bit closer to me, making his disappointment quite visible.

"What happened?" he asks.

I don't want to talk about this, but I owe him an explanation.

I wish Mom weren't so discreet and that this didn't come to him as a surprise as it did for the rest of the audience.

"Yesterday, everything was fine. We were in love. I thought that we were going to spend the rest of our lives together."

"And today?"

"Today it feels like he's a stranger."

"What happened?"

"I found out that he's cheating on me. He has been seeing his boss since three years before we got together. He says that it's nothing serious. She's married. About a year ago, they got back together and started fooling around at the office again. I walked in on them today at lunch."

My dad nods his head slightly and leans back against the chair. I don't know what he's going to say.

I only just found out that he has been on the other side of this conversation with his own wife, apparently on more than one occasion. There's a strong possibility that he'll try to make excuses for Alex.

“You shouldn’t marry him,” Dad says without a moment of hesitation. “Men like that don't change. I should know. I'm one of them.”

I shake my head.

I can't believe what he's saying to me. Suddenly tears start to bubble up at the back of my eyes and explode onto the surface.

“There's no need to cry,” he says, putting his arm around me.

I don't know why I'm crying. It has been quite an emotional day, but somehow his support in all this means everything. He's the last person that I ever thought would understand and yet, here he is, standing and taking my back despite everything.

“Your mother and I have had quite a complicated relationship,” Dad continues. “I love her, always have, but there's another part of me that nothing is ever enough. I never have enough clients, enough money, enough success. That thinking spills over into my personal life.”

I’ve never heard my father talk like this…with so much self-awareness.

"It's not that I don't love your mother. It's

just that sometimes I want more. I know that's selfish. I know that I'm hurting her. I can promise her that I will never hurt her again and that's true when I say that, but then I can't help myself. My intentions are good but I don't have the best impulse control."

My father has never been this honest with me about anything. Frankly, I had no idea that he was even capable of so much self-reflection. I'm about to say something, but then his phone rings.

"Think about what I said, Emma. You deserve to be with someone who cares about you and doesn't make you question your worth. I don't think you'll find that with Alex," he says and answers it.

17

EMMA

I sleep over at Brooke's apartment in Santa Monica and, in the morning, she wants to go to the beach. Today is Friday, a workday, but I'm off because we had plans to celebrate our engagement in Laguna Beach.

Normally, I love the beach, even though the beaches in Southern California can be a little bit windy and not that warm most of the year. The morning is overcast and breezy, a typical morning by the water, and all I want to do is stay buried under the blankets in her spare room.

Brooke has other plans.

Even though she's heavier than I am, she

loves to work out and exercise. She runs a few hours a week, usually in the morning, right when she wakes up. She also does a number of classes at the gym.

I also have a gym membership, but the few times that I go, I pick the hours that are least popular with the locals, so nothing during the early morning or early evening. I feel embarrassed about how my stomach moves when I walk on the treadmill and the fact that my face gets really red after even just a little bit of cardiovascular work.

None of that seems to bother Brooke in the least. At least not anymore.

It's a little bit after ten and she's back from yoga, where she is undoubtably the largest person there. She's smiling and invigorated just like she usually is after a hard workout.

When we were growing up, I was able to confide in Brooke about how I felt about my body, but recently I just feel embarrassed about not loving myself enough. She is all about positivity and acceptance. Somehow being unable to accept myself makes me feel worse.

Brooke's two-bedroom apartment is a few blocks from the water, near Montana and the Promenade. Her street has a number of boutique eateries, little cute clothing shops, and even a cycling store. Santa Monica doesn't look like a very high-end city, at least that's the image that it cultivates, but this two-bedroom costs our dad close to $4,000 a month. I don't think that she contributes much to the rent, but we have never really talked about it. The one thing that she knows is that I don't take any money from our parents.

"Okay," I say, finally caving to her demands while we eat a lush breakfast of pancakes and maple syrup. "We can go to the beach if you help me do some research on D. B. Carter first. It's really stressing me out, the fact that I have to turn in something on Monday and I have nothing. If I don't get the story right, she's probably going to fire me."

"She can't fire you over one story," Brooke says.

She is well aware of my relationship with Corrin and everything that has happened, but it doesn't seem like she is fully comprehending the extent of the situation.

"Corrin has been looking for a reason to get rid of me for a long time. If I can't deliver the story or at least show her that I have done a good amount of work on it, then she is just going to fire me and say that it's because I've been so preoccupied with my wedding."

Feeling flustered, I shovel a pancake into my mouth and try to make the woes of my failed relationship go away through food. Brooke gets on the computer and does some research. She counts up all of the publications that D. B. Carter has on Amazon and delivers the verdict. 152 books.

"How long has he been publishing?"

"She," Brooke corrects me. "Listen, this is a woman and you better accept that."

"Okay, she. How long has *she* been publishing?"

"It looks like it has been seven years. So, not too bad. At first there were some thrillers and more standard fantasy. Then in the last couple years, she has mainly been focusing on urban and epic fantasy," Brooke says.

I open my computer and we try to balance both laptops and our plates on the small marble table in her kitchen. After a few moments, I give up and place my MacBook on my lap. I check the messages that I have sent to D. B. Carter asking to meet. They all go unanswered, but perhaps not unread.

"Listen," Brooke says, the sun just coming out and her pointing to the few rays of sunshine peeking in through the blinds. "Let's take advantage of this and get some nice photos on the beach. I promise I'll help you do some more research when we get back."

"No," I say. "You go. I'll just stay here."

"Come with me. It will do you some good to get some fresh air."

She's right.

I want to fight her on it, but I can't.

I don't have the energy.

I head to the guest room and slip on a pair of pants and a hoodie over my T-shirt. It's in the mid-60s, but the wind can be brutal so I don't risk it. Besides, with the hoodie wrapped around me, it gives me a little bit more opportunity to mope.

We walk to the beach and Brooke starts taking a few outside shots of whatever's in front of her. There's a bread store that puts out fresh baked loaves in the window. They look so delicious that my mouth actually waters looking at them. Brooke snaps a picture of them and then one of her pointing to them in a selfie for her Instagram stories.

"You seem to like taking photos a lot," I say. "Have you ever thought about doing something in photography?"

"Actually, I have. A friend of mine asked me to photograph her wedding. The only problem is that I don't have a good camera. Those Cannon ones go for a grand."

"Did you ask Dad?"

"I did. He said to ask him again after the engagement party. Apparently, he spent a lot on it."

I roll my eyes and she laughs.

"You know that I had nothing to do with that party, right?"

"Of course! You don't think that I know

you? That old party was just all about Mom and Lindsey celebrating themselves. You were the guest of honor, but no one gave a damn about what you wanted."

"Yeah," I say quietly. "If they did, then there wouldn't be any toasts and I wouldn't have to announce to 200 people that my fiancé is a fucking cheater and a liar."

"I'm really sorry about that," she says, taking my hand in hers and giving me a squeeze.

When we get to the beach, we walk past the monkey bars. There's a ridiculously hot guy with eight pack abs doing upside down crunches. This is a change from the usual when there are guys with only six pack abs doing pull-ups.

Brooke points to him, but I have my eye on someone else. It suddenly occurs to me that since I'm no longer engaged or even in a relationship that these men are an actual option for me.

Brooke continues to take selfies of herself in various poses. She brought a few changes of outfits in her oversized tote bag and layers them one after the other, removing the one underneath to vary the shots. Underneath it all, she's wearing a two piece.

"You mind snapping a few pictures?" she asks, forcing me to look up from my Kindle in the middle of a very exciting part in the story.

"I don't really want to," I say.

"Come on, please," she begs.

I let out a deep sigh, scramble up to my feet, and take her phone. She tells me exactly where to stand and how to shoot it. Then she points her face, tilting her chin and maximizing her eyes. Her elbows are in opposite directions and her body is curved to minimize the waist and accentuate her breasts.

I can't help but admire her confidence. It seems to come so naturally to her, almost like breathing and no matter what I do, I can't make myself feel that way.

After I hand her back her phone, a smile comes over her face as she looks through the pictures and then she lets out a squeal.

"He texted me back!"

18

EMMA

As soon as Brooke shows me the phone, it takes me a few moments to realize that she's talking about Liam from the party.

Immediately, I feel annoyed.

It was nice to meet you yesterday, Liam texts. Brooke shows me the phone and squeals giddily.

Yeah, me, too, she texts back.

She waits for him to say something else, but he doesn't.

We walk back from the beach and my skin feels salty from the air.

She asks me how I feel about her

possibly asking out Liam and I, of course, tell her that that's totally fine.

"I just know that you two talked earlier in the night and I wasn't sure if you…"

She lets her voice trail off.

I shake my head vigorously.

"I'm not into guys, right now. Maybe not ever."

I tell her this, but it's a lie. That's the thing about a crush, it happens whether you want it to or not.

I wouldn't go so far as to call it a crush, but there is something about Liam that has intrigued me. He has the kind of honesty that seems quite rare nowadays and I appreciate that.

Brooke points to her phone, but no new text messages arrive.

"Why would he just text me that and then not say anything else?" she asks.

"I have no idea."

I forgot how much energy women spend analyzing text messages and what men have said or not said in them. Every comma, every emoji, or lack thereof gets analyzed for critical reasoning like an English paper quality standard assessment.

On the way back to her place, we pop into an Indian restaurant that makes the most delicious curry and put in an order to go.

While we wait, Brooke obsesses about Liam and I try to change the topic of conversation.

I pull out my phone and do some more research on D. B. Carter.

There are a number of Facebook groups devoted to discussing his work and I join all of them. There are also a number of forums that discuss his books and I make an account there to try to get some more information about where I can find him.

Once the Facebook group moderators accept me, I scour through the posts. Most of them are dedicated to gushing about the work, but there are a few people who wonder about the writer's identity and how it is that he can put out so many books so quickly.

I ask Brooke about that and she shrugs

and tells me that it's actually not that uncommon.

"Really? Do people really publish this many books?"

"Yes, you'd be surprised. Check out Bella Forrest or just about any other successful indie writer in the romance genre. Even Willow Rose, who writes thrillers. She has more than seventy-five books, at last count. Some people are really prolific and basically that's the thing that builds their brand and gets their readers to come back. Some people publish a book a month and they are quality, good books and their readers appreciate that."

"Readers like you?" I ask.

She shrugs her shoulders and says, "Of course. You know me, I like to read a lot. It seems like nowadays, in the age of Netflix, what's the point of just reading one book if that's what you want to do for entertainment? The author I read has to have a big catalog so that I can really devote myself to their series."

I agree with her. I hadn't really thought about the importance of publishing a lot in order to build a brand, but it makes perfect sense.

There's so much competition and there're so many writers out there that the way to get people interested in you and to devote their reading time to your book is to have a lot of books published.

"Have you ever thought about writing anything?" she asks. "I mean besides articles?"

I shrug.

It would be a lie to say that I haven't.

Of course I have.

A number of times.

I actually managed to write about 20,000 words of a novel before I couldn't figure out what to do with the rest of the story and gave up.

"I know that you are a really good reporter and that you enjoy that kind of work, but I thought that maybe you would like to write some fiction as well."

"Yeah," I say, shaking my head. "It's kind of crazy to think about but why not, right? I'm just worried that no one would read anything that I would want to write," I add jokingly.

"I think the attitude that you have to have is that you have to do it until."

"Until what?"

"Just until. People will probably not like your first books. Hell, you'll be lucky to even find anyone to read them, but if you take the long-term view and decide for yourself that you'll keep going until then you'll keep getting better. Better at writing. Better at marketing. Better at everything."

Brooke pays for the food and I grab the bags.

She looks down at her phone to see if maybe Liam has texted back, but he hasn't.

I let out a sigh of relief.

19

LIAM

I don't have Emma's contact info, but I do have her sister's. We had a nice conversation, but I also don't want to send her the wrong message.

I don't know why my thoughts keep focusing on Emma. She's the last girl that I should be thinking about.

Alex is a lot of things and he has a lot of flaws, but he's also a friend. Emma is his significant other. Maybe she's not engaged to him anymore but whatever is happening between them, it's very new and very raw and I can't let myself think about her.

It's early morning when I climb out of

bed and immediately slip on my running shoes. I haven't always been a runner, but I've gotten into quite a funk over the last few months and the only way out is to actually wake up and force myself to go.

When I was in high school, up in Seattle, I used to be on the track team. I ran hurdles and the two-mile run. I even did cross country. Long distance running was never my thing, but I always wanted to do a marathon.

I step outside of the hotel and turn on my watch. I've been tracking my mileage, however embarrassingly minimal.

I try not to think about it.

Just set the watch to an outdoor run and put one foot in front of the other, I say to myself.

My hotel is small and boutique-like, with no rooms under $500 a night. There's a nice pool and a hot tub as well, but it's in the low 60s in Santa Monica and filled entirely by out-of-staters.

The breeze coming off the ocean feels good against my skin. It wakes me up even if I don't want to.

There's a road going above the cliff with a view of the ocean, but I take the steps down and run along the water line. The sand is dark brown, almost gray, matching the early morning weather.

It's not warm, but it's not cold either.

The humidity makes the air thick and I manage to run without struggling for breath for over a mile and a half. Pushing myself hard, I feel the roaring of my muscles with each step.

Running out here feels so different from running back home. It's not just the sand under my feet, providing additional resistance and making my muscles work harder.

It's more than that.

The city is full of people. Most not awake yet, but I know that they will be emerging out of their apartments soon. So far, there are a few occasional homeless people walking with their bags of stuff in the park just near the ocean.

I swallow hard and remember my own life back on the streets in San Francisco. I had just graduated from college and I needed to get away from life. I had worked hard all of my life.

I did everything that I was supposed to do and I'd had enough. Maybe I read *Into the Wild* with Christopher McCandless a few too many times, but I was inspired to strike out on my own. I didn't have many material possessions. I gave up my apartment and I paid off the last of my debts on my credit cards.

I packed a small bag and drove down from Seattle all along the coast.

Instead of sleeping in hotel rooms or short-term rentals, I slept in my car. The first few nights were difficult and uncomfortable, but I had my books to protect me from all the evils in the world.

Books and music, that's all I needed back then.

When I got to San Francisco, I parked my car in long-term parking and made my way around the city. I knew that I wasn't really destitute the way that many of the people were out there. I wasn't abandoned by my family. I didn't have mental health problems. I was a tourist. I was there to see what life was really like.

What was it like?

It was hard, cold, and without much comfort.

The days were too long and the nights were even longer. I met a few friends, but then they didn't turn out to be that friendly at all. One of them stole my bag and another stole my wallet. It was then that I decided that city life wasn't for me.

I managed to get back to my car where I had some money stowed away. Then I drove south. I drove until I got to Santa Barbara. I walked into the first restaurant they had on the beach and asked for a job. I needed money to get by and they needed a server to charm the ladies. I was good at that.

Don't get me wrong. I'm well aware of my privilege. I made a choice to go on that trip and to live on the streets. Most of the people out there do not.

Once things got a little bit hard, I got back into my car and I tried out something different. I applied for a job and got it on the spot. That probably had a lot to do with the fact that I was young, attractive, and well-spoken.

Still, I continued to live in my car. I read my books and tried to figure out what to do with my life. I knew that I couldn't go back to see my family, but I also didn't want to be a server for the rest of my life. I had a four-year degree, but I didn't want to have a nine-to-five job.

Besides, there was something else that I wanted to do. The only thing, really.

When I get to the two-mile mark, I bend in half trying to catch my breath. My phone buzzes. Running in the sand is a whole other thing from running on hard ground. Both are uneven, but back home there are hundreds of rocks that can sprain your ankle, here the sand feels like it's practically pulling you down inside of itself.

I click on the message app. It's Brooke. I contacted her for only one reason, to get in touch with her sister and now I don't want to write her back.

We had a nice talk last night. I was

friendly, but it was Emma that kept me up all night. It is Emma that I can't stop thinking about.

I take a deep breath and turn around. A seagull flies over my head and lands on the waves, plunging her head into the water.

Three surfers walk up behind me, laughing. They are dressed in thick neoprene suits, with only their heads exposed. The youngest one, who looks about twelve, pulls the hood over his head to keep extra warm. Even though the temperature is mildly warm in Southern California most of the year, the water comes from Alaska and it rarely gets into the mid-60s, even during the height of summer.

I lean over carefully to avoid the waves and scoop up a little bit into the palm of my hand. It's ice cold and when I throw it on my face, it cools me off immediately.

I take a deep breath and turn up the music on my headphones. Then I start to run.

Later that morning, I pick up the phone and text Brooke.

As soon as she replies, I want to ask her for Emma's number, but I decide against it.

Instead, I don't write her again.

20

EMMA

I spend the afternoon alone.

Luckily, Brooke has a lunch date with a few of her friends. She invites me to join them, but I decline.

At first, she says that she'll stay and hang out with me, but I tell her that I want to be alone.

It's true.

I need a lot of downtime. I'm not one of those people that can just go from social event to social event and get replenished from having contact with other people.

Before I found Alex cheating on me, I was looking forward to spending the weekend with just him and my Kindle. I thought that we would swim, order room service, make love, and then just hang out each doing our own thing.

I'm still trying to process everything that happened.

After I found him cheating on me, I should have gone home and climbed under the covers and stayed there. After all, that's exactly what I wanted to do. The party changed all that.

Now? I don't know, maybe going to the party was a good thing.

I miss him, of course.

My heart is broken.

I want him back and I also want him dead.

It's hard to explain what it feels like to wake up one morning and have everything in your life different. The one person that I thought that I could trust is gone. What am I left with?

Don't be like that, Emma, I say to myself. You have a lot of things to be grateful for. You have a job you love. You have people who care about you.

You're well-off, and even if you yourself

aren't particularly well-off, the fact is that your family is. There're so many people in the world, in fact the vast majority, that are not in your situation. It doesn't mean that you can't feel sorry for yourself, but it does mean that you should keep things in perspective.

When I feel myself spiraling into a hole of depression, I decide to do something proactive. I have the apartment to myself so I pour myself a big mug of tea, grab a bar of chocolate, and sit on Brooke's thick, upholstered couch that probably cost Dad more than just a few thousand dollars.

I put my laptop on my knees and start reading the messages in search of D. B. Carter. A few people in the Facebook groups have replied to my queries, the majority of whom say nothing of importance. Most are only interested in talking about his books, but one person by the name of Matt Lipinski mentions that D. B. Carter lives in Pioneertown, California.

I immediately friend Matt and message him about his post. When I look up Pioneertown on Google, I discover that it's a dusty desert town about two and half hours east of Los Angeles.

It's about twenty-five minutes away from the famous Joshua Tree National Park. The thing that it's most famous for is a restaurant/bar called Pappy and Harriet's, which is a small venue but has had the likes of Paul McCartney and other famous rock musicians perform there.

Its other claim to fame is the town itself, which looks like an old Western movie set. There's a saloon, a little white church, and a number of weathered-wood shops selling turquoise jewelry and handmade horse saddles.

A few minutes later, I get a message from Matt.

What makes you think that D. B. Carter lives in Pioneertown? I write.

I really shouldn't say, he texts back after a moment.

I would really love the opportunity to contact him or her.

For a moment, I wonder if I'm actually talking to D. B. Carter in real life. Stranger things have happened.

In case I am, I add, *I just want to do a small interview. If D. B. Carter isn't interested then I'm not going to write an article at all, but I haven't had any luck contacting him or her directly through social media.*

Should you take that as a hint? Matt asks.

My heart sinks.

I click on Matt's name and examine the avatar of a spaceship. We are not friends and he does not accept my friend request.

The only things that I have access to are the profile pictures and they all feature different science-fiction images including a cover of one of D. B. Carter's books from a few years back.

I'm not really sure if the messages are getting through to him, I say, now almost certain that Matt is D. B. Carter, or at the very least a family member or friend.

Okay, Matt says. *Here's the address: 10745 Old West Ln.*

I shake my head. This has to be a joke.

I'm about to write something back, but not before first putting the address into Google. Much to my surprise, he leads me to Zillow where I see that this house was purchased two years ago for $2.45 million.

I furrow my brow, not wanting to believe what I have just discovered. There's no name listed as the owner and that will require a little bit more research.

In the meantime, I turn back to Matt and text: *Do you really expect me to believe that D. B. Carter lives in almost a 2 1/2 million dollar house in an old West town?*

Believe whatever you want.

Do you happen to have a phone number where I could reach him?

I wait for him to write me back, but all I get is crickets.

21

EMMA

Matt Lipinski, a.k.a. D. B. Carter, does not get in touch with me again.

I decide that's his name, but I'm only 50% certain.

He must be fucking with me, right? I mean why would he lurk on these Facebook groups and then reveal his name to me, a reporter, of all people?

No, this must be a joke.

I think about it for a long time, putting my computer away and stopping the search.

I have an address, but no idea what I should do with it. Brooke comes home later that evening and I tell her what happened.

She shakes her head and then says, "There's no way that it could be him. The only thing that's going to happen here is that we waste a day driving three hours all the way to Joshua Tree to disturb some random family who lives there. Do you really want to do that?"

I hate to admit it, but yes.

I know that the likelihood of that address belonging to D. B. Carter is quite slim, but I don't care.

Matt might be making fun of me or playing a game, but I also don't care.

"Why don't you go with me? We can make it a little road trip."

"I'd love to, but I have a photography session set up for tomorrow."

"If I do this, then I can only go tomorrow. I'll need to use Sunday to write up some sort of report."

Brooke orders some Thai food on her phone and then turns to me.

"This is why you're doing this? You want to show your boss the lengths that you will go to uncover this mystery. You know that she's not going to appreciate it, right? Nothing you do will be enough."

I shrug. She's right. I know that and she knows that.

"No, this isn't about that," I say.

My phone goes off and I look at the screen.

It's Liam, the guy that I met at the party.

He has messaged me on Instagram. I click on his profile. It doesn't seem to be very active. A few pictures here and there, most of landscapes with a few selfies.

Most of them are pictures of him running.

Hey, how are you doing? He writes in a direct message.

I know that he contacted Brooke earlier and I wonder if he's writing me to get in touch with her. But why? She wrote him back and it was he who didn't respond.

"What's up?" Brooke walks over and glances down at my phone.

I quickly close the app before she's able to see, but the moment feels suspicious.

I know that she likes Liam a lot, but I think I might, too. Of course, my situation is a little complicated given the fact that I am only un-engaged for a day, but it doesn't change the fact that I'm intrigued.

What is it that people say about rebounds? You have to go through them in order to find the one that you really want.

I didn't really believe any of that before, but now it hits a little bit too close to home.

Suddenly, I get this overwhelming feeling of needing to be wanted. Like most couples, Alex and I had fallen into a groove with our intimacy. It had its ebbs and flows.

It was never completely gone, but it wasn't like it was when we first met.

Then, walking into his office and seeing *them* together? Something changed within me.

Suddenly, I had this overwhelming need to prove that someone wants me.

Maybe that's all that's happening with Liam.

Maybe we didn't really have a connection.

Maybe I was just intrigued by the attention that he paid me.

That evening, I make the decision that

early the following morning, I'm going to drive out to the desert. I try to contact Matt a few more times, but all my messages go unanswered.

I scour other forums and posts, but no one else has a clue or volunteers any information.

"This is the only thing I have to do," I tell Brooke that night when we split a bottle of wine. "If I go out there and it's just a ruse and an Internet joke, then so be it. At least I'll spend some time in the car thinking about everything that has happened. If I don't go out there, then I'll always wonder *what if*? What if by some slim chance Matt is actually D. B. Carter? What if by some chance he is actually interested in giving me an interview and this is some sort of test?"

22

LIAM

Alex and I meet up for lunch since we didn't get much of a chance to talk last night. I haven't seen him in a while and am frankly surprised that he called me up and invited me out.

I meet him downtown, not far from where he works.

"I thought that you were going to take off today," I say when the server seats us at a table with a white tablecloth and takes our drink order.

He shrugs and looks down at the menu.

There's a nervousness to him, that I don't remember from growing up. He was always the alpha guy, confident, self-assured.

"Well, Emma and I had planned to spend the weekend in Laguna Beach, but she hasn't been returning my calls so I decided to head back to work."

"Why not just stay home?"

"What's the point? The only thing that makes sense in my life is my work."

I give him a slight nod.

"So, what is it that you do?" I ask. "I mean, I know that you're in finance, but what does that entail exactly?"

Alex raises one of his eyebrows and gives me a look as if to say, *I thought that you would never ask.* Then he launches into a long discussion about his father's hedge fund and his role as one of its top directors.

"I know that over email you mentioned that you possibly wanted to invest some money with us," Alex says. "Is that still the case?"

I give him a nod. I'm keenly aware of the fact that he hasn't asked me what I do for a living yet and I wonder how long it's going to take him.

"How much are you thinking?" Alex asks.

"I'm not really sure," I say, moving my hands out of the way to allow the server to place two glasses of scotch on the rocks in front of us.

After we order, Alex raises his glass and makes a toast.

"It's nice to have you back in my life. It has been way too long."

"Hey, thanks for inviting me," I say, hitting my drink with his.

The thick expensive glasses make a loud reverberating echo. I bring it to my lips and revel in the oak colored liquid running down the back of my throat.

"So, I don't think I ever asked, but what kind of work are you in?"

I think about my answer carefully. I don't want to lie, but I don't want to come out with the whole truth either.

Hardly anyone knows and I'd like to keep it that way.

"I've been doing a lot of day trading. I've gotten quite good at it so my nest egg kind of grew. I like it because it frees me up to do a lot of other stuff in my life like woodworking, camping, hiking, reading, that sort of thing."

"Oh my God, man. It's like you're retired," Alex says.

At first, I take it as an insult, but I quickly realize that he doesn't mean it that way at all. He's looking at me with admiration.

"I wish that I could do something like that with my life," Alex says, finishing his drink and waving over to the server for another. "Don't get me wrong, I like my job, but it gets stressful."

"You know, you don't have to work all those hours. You could take it easy. Everyone needs a little bit of self-care, isn't that what they're calling it these days?"

"Self-care? What the hell is that?" Alex asks. "I work over 100 hours a week and if I don't, then I'll have to work 150 hours the next one. Is there even that many in week?"

"So, that's all you do? Work?"

"Yup, pretty much. These three days off would have been the first days that I have taken off since Emma and I met. Wow, I can't believe that it has been that long."

Our food arrives.

Alex ordered oysters and a lobster tail. He digs into it feverishly as soon as it arrives. I'm not very hungry but the taco salad with avocado and green onions is delicious. It's also huge, much bigger than I thought it would be, taking up almost half the table.

I finish my scotch and order another round. At this point, Alex is on drink number four, but who's counting?

"So, you never told me about how much you were thinking of investing." Alex brings the conversation back to the basics.

I take a big bite and chew, debating whether I should tell him the truth.

"I have a few investments in real estate but have more liquid investments in the stock market. I think I'd like to allocate… Two million."

When he hears the amount, he chokes on his food.

I smile at the corner of my lips and take another sip of the smooth and delicious scotch from the top shelf.

"Wait, seriously?" Alex asks after a moment.

I shrug.

"Are you serious?" he asks, putting his hand over my knuckles.

I nod.

"Okay, dude, you totally made it sound like you were just a day trader, not like you had actual serious money."

I shrug, taking a bite of my salad.

"I'm not sure what you wanted me to-" I start to say, but he puts his finger in my face, shaking his head.

"You showed up at the party dressed, pretty subpar, to be honest."

"What are you talking about? I was wearing a suit."

"Oh, come on. I know suits. That one didn't even cost 400 bucks."

I laugh.

"Are you seriously telling me that you're one of those secretly wealthy guys that just goes around dressing like a normal person?"

I continue to laugh. I find his shock to be purely comical.

"Okay," I say, clearing my throat. "Yes, I am wealthy, but I'm not hiding that fact. I just like to wear what I like to wear and not wear what I don't like to wear. I'm not much like you guys. I got the first suit that I saw at the department store and it helped that it also had a nice fit."

"No." Alex shakes his head. "That was… Okay. You mostly looked nice because you have a killer body and it was a slim fit, but as far as suits go, it was pretty crappy."

The more that we banter back and forth, the more relaxed I start to feel. There was a time when Alex and I were close. He was one of the most popular kids in school and I was the kind of kid who had friends in a lot of cliques.

I was a theater kid and the jock. Somehow it all worked out. But people loved Alex. When my family moved to Seattle at the end of middle school, I missed him the most.

At first, we stayed in touch on the phone and Skype, but after a while… You know how kids are.

"Okay, be honest with me," Alex says, ordering another drink and slurring his words just a little bit.

I nod and wait.

"Weren't you like, living on the streets at one point? How did you go from there to this?"

I shrug and say, "I was interested in finding some work that I could do on a freelance sort of basis. I wanted to go rock climbing, camping, traveling, and stuff like that. I wanted to make money, but I didn't want it to consume my life. That's when trading sort of came about and the more that I found out about it, the more interested I got."

This is all true, but it's not the whole truth. I have been doing some day trading, but there's a whole other part of my life I'm never going to share.

"So, tell me about Emma," I say, changing the subject.

"What do you want to know?" The tone of his voice changes immediately to something callused and distant.

"What the hell happened?"

He shrugs and says, "Women, you know?"

I hate statements like that. They're

misogynistic, self-serving, and only used by men who don't know how to communicate.

"No, I don't," I say, leaning back in my chair.

The server takes our plates away and offers us the dessert menu. I surprise myself by ordering a vegan cheesecake on a whim. Not just because it's vegan, but because I'm not much of a dessert person.

"I don't know why she came to see me at lunch yesterday. She wasn't supposed to. She walked in on me with Jen."

"Jen?"

"Jennifer Lester, my immediate superior."

I nod, trying to look surprised.

"I know. I'm such an asshole," Alex says, slurring his words.

He's had so many drinks in such a short time that I'm actually shocked that he's still speaking coherently, but he has a high tolerance.

"How long have you been seeing her?" I ask.

"A while," he says, biting his lower lip.

"We were together for three years before I met Emma."

"Wow, that long?"

"Uh-huh."

I wait for him to offer me something else, but he doesn't.

"So, why aren't you and Jen together?"

"Don't you think that I want to be? She is off limits."

I tilt my head, waiting for him to explain.

"Jen is married. Not happily, but they have two kids together who are nine and seven. She made it clear to me on numerous occasions that she has no plans to file for divorce and to uproot her children. In fact, she's perfectly fine with just keeping our relationship exclusively to the office."

"Shit. I'm sorry," I say, shaking my head.

"I tried to stop. When I first met Emma, I broke up with Jen. I wanted a clean slate. I got tired of being in this… Unfulfilling relationship."

I can see his pain, just below the surface.

"The thing is that," he continues, "Jen and I work insane hours. Her husband understands that and I thought that Emma did, too. Before I met Emma, Jen and I were together all the time. All mornings, all afternoons, and all nights. We would fool around and then we'd get back to work. She had no reason to leave her husband because she barely saw him as is, but she also really wanted to keep her children in a stable home."

I nod my head, trying to think of something to say.

"You know, women have been in these situations with men for millennia," I finally say. "That's why there's even that cliché about sleeping with your married boss and expecting him to leave his family for you."

"Of course," Alex says, shaking his head. "I know that. I'm a fool for wishing that she would choose me. I'm a fool for leading Emma along and then going back to Jen. I just love her."

I give him a slight nod and then ask, "Who? Who do you love?"

"Um, Je-" he starts to say, but then catches himself. "I love Emma, of course."

"What do you think is going to happen

now?" I ask and reach for the bill, but he grabs it out of my hand.

"Listen, I have all intentions of signing you as a client so why don't you just let me pay for this. We can call this a potential investor meeting."

"Let me get this straight," I say with a smirk. "I give you $2 million of my money to manage and in exchange you treat me to a $400 lunch? Yep, that seems fair."

"I don't see what's wrong with that at all," Alex says and puts his business credit card in the folder with the bill.

23

EMMA

I haven't taken a long drive in a while and I've never taken one by myself before. Part of me was afraid of coming out here alone, so I kept trying to get Brooke to go with me, but as soon as I get into the car, I realize that it's a good thing that she refused.

I get on the freeway early in the morning.

There are still a lot of cars even though it is Saturday, but they start to thin out after Pasadena. It has been on my bucket list to go out to Joshua Tree National Park and this is my chance. I'm going to pop into Pioneertown which is about twenty-five minutes east of the park and if D. B. Carter isn't there, I will just keep driving and head to the park. I'll salvage the day however I can.

For a long time, I drive in silence.

I know that a lot of people like to listen to the radio or an audiobook, but it feels good just to look around and think. When I first started this drive, my hands were sweaty and I was gripping the wheel tightly. As the minutes ticked away, I started to relax.

About an hour and a half into the drive, I pull into a gas station to use the restroom. I'm tempted to stop by the snack aisles and pick out something junkie to nibble on, but I'm proud of myself when I get back in the car without making a purchase.

My thoughts keep swirling around Alex and the mysterious writer that I'm certain I will not be able to find. I started one of his books last night and ended up staying up half the night.

I'm not much of a fantasy fan, but the realism that was infused into each scene made me connect with the story and kept me turning pages.

The book ended on a cliffhanger and of course I had to buy the next one immediately. In addition to the book, I also purchased the audiobook and downloaded it. When I get back into the car, I turn on the Bluetooth and pair it to my phone.

The story opens with a sexy scene where the two main characters finally get together and have sex for the first time. The words flowing out from my speakers are eloquent, precise, and incredibly arousing. When traffic slows down near the Ontario airport, I actually feel my cheeks blushing as I look around, hoping that none of the other drivers can hear the audio in my car.

I have never read romance before.

Is this what it is really like?

Shit, no wonder everyone loves it.

Suddenly, I realize how unnatural some of the books that I have previously enjoyed are when the author ends the scene with two people falling into bed together and fading to black.

If it's something that happens, why not go into it?

Why not offer the details and describe it

just as you do a car chase or just about anything else? We all want to know.

I finish the book and start another, which is also heavy on both fantasy and romance and with a good dose of sexy scenes that makes my mouth water. By the time I pull into Yucca Valley and see the sign to Pioneertown, I have to turn it off to try to focus on why I'm here.

The beauty of the desert is undeniable.

There are enormous boulders and tall leaning cacti springing up from the hills and valleys with an almost endless blue sky up above.

Whatever clouds hovered over Santa Monica have all burned off. Out here, the sky is huge and my mind clears immediately.

Suddenly, I don't feel this oppression of thought as if something from the heavens is pushing down on me. There are no low hanging clouds, just a bright and unforgivable sun.

The road leading up to Pioneertown is winding surrounded by enormous boulders. When I get to the top of the hill, I see the famous Pappy and Harriet's and all of the

Harley-Davidson motorcycles parked in a neat row in front.

I've never been to a biker bar before so I promise myself that no matter what happens today, I'm going to come back here and have lunch. My stomach rumbles and I consider having some lunch before going to the house, but I'm too nervous to prolong this meeting anymore than I absolutely have to.

Driving to the parking lot behind the restaurant, I pull up next to the dusty unmarked main street of the Old West town and look at the big sign that prohibits cars from driving through.

Proceed on foot or horseback only

I slow down and look out of the window at the little shops selling turquoise jewelry. One of the places has a big leather saddle out front, the exact one that I saw in my Instagram search.

There's also supposedly a church and a saloon further down the dusty road, but I don't get out of my car to investigate. I drive back out onto the paved road and let GPS lead me to my address. If this is all fake and there is no writer living at this house, then I'll have plenty of time to tour the town.

The directions lead me a few miles down the road and then instruct me to turn left up an unpaved, desert path. There's a dip and the bottom of my car scrapes along the ground.

I consider parking and then walking the rest of the way, but I don't see the house from here and according to the GPS, it's another few miles away. That's a long walk under the hot desert sun so I get back into the car and keep driving.

A very bumpy two miles later, I reach a wrought iron gate, placed almost arbitrarily in the middle of the road. If I were in a different type of vehicle, I could easily drive around it and onto the property, but there are cacti, shrubs, and all sorts of other vegetation blocking my way. I get out of the car and look for the button to call the owner.

There isn't one.

I walk around and put my hand over my forehead to block some of the sun, peering into the distance. There, on top of the hill, I see the house sitting on at least five acres of property.

The gate doesn't have a way to call, but it also doesn't have a lock so when I pull up one of the latches it swings inward, welcoming me inside.

Back home, I would not have dared to walk through a gate without first trying to reach the owner because I know that they will call the police.

Out here?

The consequences are probably more dire. I'm pretty certain that almost everyone owns a gun and isn’t afraid to use it.

But I get into my car and drive over anyway.

The house is a modern masterpiece. It’s made entirely of glass resembling those rectangular mansions they have scattered over the Hollywood Hills.

I park my car out front and walk down the carefully manicured desert landscaped yard full of barrel and saguaro cacti.

When I step on a twig, it cracks underneath my foot. A black crow takes off from the roof, startling me.

I take a deep breath and look up at the couple of stairs leading to the enormous distressed wood double doors, which look more like an entrance to a castle than a single-family home in the desert.

There's a small doorbell to one side and when I press it, an antique sounding bell reverberates throughout the house. A dog runs up to one of the windows adjoining the doors just as I peek through. All I spot is the large foyer before a toy Australian Shepherd jumps up on her hind legs and launches herself at the window, barking her head off.

The dog is gray, white, and orange, with the bluest eyes you have ever seen. She barks loudly and proudly and doesn't let up. When I dare to touch the glass, she stands up even taller and presses her paws harder into the glass.

I wait for a few moments. I don't need to ring the doorbell again or use the enormous door knocker. If anyone is home, this dog has done a lot to notify them of the fact that I'm here.

Ten minutes later, still no one answers.

I wait in the yard, away from the front

door and the dog eventually gives up and lies down. The few times that I decided to step on the porch, she jumps up and tells me to go away.

I'm not sure what to do. Clearly, someone lives here and they're not home, but I don't know when they are going to be back.

I also have no idea if this is the person that I'm looking for.

Probably not.

I am hesitant to walk around the property, but my curiosity gets the best of me. There are sharp, futuristic looking Joshua trees all around leading to a wonderland of enormous granite boulders.

Turning the corner, I peek over one side and see that the whole back of the house is an enormous piece of glass. There seems to be no walls and no separation between the living room and the towering, twenty-foot rock outcroppings out back. The landscape is otherworldly and reminds me of a time when dinosaurs roamed.

Suddenly, far in the distance near the horizon, I see someone trotting on a horse.

24

EMMA

It's 10 o'clock and the sun is not at its highest point in the sky yet, but it's already beaming down a curtain of heat.

I peer into the distance, straining my neck, to get a better look at the silhouette of the man riding his horse. Sitting comfortably in the saddle as if he belongs there, he lifts up his hand to adjust his cowboy hat.

I look closer. I even pull up my sunglasses to the top of my head, but the blinding light makes it hard to see.

There is a narrow path meandering between the boulders stacked near the house and the horse expertly makes her way toward me.

I know that I'm not supposed to be out here on his property, in his backyard, but I can't make myself move.

When they get closer to the house, the man's face remains in shadow under the wide-brimmed hat and I can't quite make out his face.

The horse, on the other hand, is absolutely magnificent. She is tall and elegant and her coat glistens with sweat. She is the color of chestnut with a long oak mane and deep, curious eyes. When the man squeezes his legs, she trots over to me, stopping a few inches away.

"Emma?" Liam asks.

My mouth drops open as I look up at him with my hand over my forehead.

"What are you doing here?" I ask.

My voice cracks in the middle, forcing me to clear my throat with a cough.

"Is everything okay?" Liam asks, jumping off the horse and taking off his hat. "Did something happen to Alex?"

Then it hits me.

He has no idea why I'm here.

How could he?

I stare at him, shaking my head, not sure how to start.

"Alex is fine," I say.

"Okay," Liam says slowly, waiting for me to explain.

"You really don't know why I'm here?"

"No."

"You didn't write that post with your address on it?"

He shakes his head no.

"You're not Matt Lipinski?"

"Who is Matt Lipinski?"

We're not getting anywhere with this and suddenly, I realize that he may not know anything about Matt at all, if that's even his name.

"So…you live here?" I ask.

"Yes, this is my house," Liam says, waving his arm. He leads the horse closer to the barn and drops her lead over a hitching post.

Then he turns to face me.

Dressed in a plain white T-shirt, tight jeans, and cowboy boots, he looks nothing like the sophisticated investor that I met in Calabasas.

I like that.

He wipes the sweat off his brow with the back of his hand.

"What are you doing here, Emma?" he asks. "How did you find out that I live here?"

I wait for a few moments and tap my foot on the ground. A little cloud of dust gathers around my flip-flop and settles on my newly painted toenails.

"Are you… D. B. Carter?" I ask.

The expression on his face changes from an awkward friendliness to something resembling dissatisfaction.

I don't know him well, but he isn't pleased.

The answer to my question must be yes.

"How did you find me?" Liam asks. "Is that why you were chatting me up at the party?"

I shake my head and say, "No. I had no idea who you were."

"Yet, you're here, at my home. How did you get my address? Alex doesn't know where I live. Alex doesn't even know what I do."

"He doesn't?" I ask.

"You need to leave," Liam says.

He turns his body away from me and starts to walk away, but I catch up with him.

Now that my shock is wearing off, I need to get some answers.

"Listen, I had no idea that you were D. B. Carter," I say. "I was assigned a story on him, this reclusive and prolific romantic fantasy author that no one knows anything about. I searched through Facebook groups and forums and finally someone just happened to message me with your address. I thought it was a joke. The only reason I came out here is just to confirm that this guy, Matt, was lying. Plus, LA was feeling a little bit claustrophobic after everything that happened."

I'm putting everything on the line and I hope that he realizes that.

I don't have any other choice.

I have a feeling that this is the only way that I can get him to talk to me.

Liam hesitates. Standing on the beautifully distressed porch in the back, he turns on the heels of his cowboy boots and faces me again.

His eyes are cast downward, but they eventually meet mine. He looks so different from the night that I first met him and yet with his hair falling in his face like that, I see the man that I can't stop thinking about.

"Who is Matt?" Liam asks after a moment.

"What?"

"You said Matt gave you my address. Who is he?"

"I have no idea," I say, shaking my head. "His name is Matt Lipinski, but that could just be a nickname or something made up. I can't remember what forum it was, but he replied to one of my questions about you and then messaged me directly and told me your address."

I repeat my story again, hoping that this time he believes it.

I watch him hesitate. He narrows his

eyes and stares at me. He doesn't believe me. My heart sinks. I'm not sure what else I can do to convince him that I'm telling the truth.

"How else could I find out your address? Nobody knows who you are. Like you said, not even Alex."

"That's by design," Liam says. "I don't want anyone knowing what I do."

"Why?" I ask.

He raises his hand in my face and asks, "You're a reporter, right?"

I nod.

"Whatever I tell you is off the record."

I let out a deep sigh.

Shit.

Those are the magic words. Now he can tell me his deepest secret like that he is actually the Golden State killer and I don't have the right to print it. At least, not ethically and not under my name.

I feel myself starting to freak out, but I take a few deep breaths and tell myself to calm down.

It doesn't matter.

So, what if everything that he says right now is off the record?

We have developed a rapport.

Maybe I can get him to change his mind.

“Okay,” I say. “It's off the record.”

Still, Liam hesitates. I lift my hands up in the air to show him that my hands are empty.

“I'm not recording anything. You can take a look at my phone,” I say, pulling it out of my back pocket. “Can I ask you something? Why don't you want anyone to know that you’re D. B. Carter? You're famous. There are millions of people around the world who love your work. Yet, no one knows who you really are.”

“You have asked and answered your own question.”

He starts to walk away and I'm not sure if I should follow him. So, I stand here, in his backyard next to his horse who is feverishly drinking from the trough.

“Your horse is beautiful,” I add as he heads up the stairs.

I see his dog through the enormous living room window, barking up a storm. Surprisingly, the house is so well insulated that I can barely hear her at all.

"Are you coming in or not?" Liam asks.

He doesn't wait for me to answer and disappears into the house.

Not wanting to push my luck, I follow him inside.

25

EMMA

The back entrance leads through a small foyer, where Liam takes off his boots and leaves them haphazardly in the middle of the floor. As soon as I walk over the threshold, the dog runs up to me, yelping, but Liam places his hand on her head, and she immediately calms down.

"This is Skylar," he says. "She's a little protective of me, but she's friendly. Don't worry, she won't bite."

I lean over to try to pet her, but she bursts out into another cacophony of barks.

"You might want to give her some time," he advises.

I decide to not approach her again until she calms down.

Liam leads me to the large kitchen island made of marble and reinforced with steel and offers me something to drink. There's a farmhouse sink with one of those modern, spring-like faucets installed in the island and when I tell him that I want some water, he grabs a Mason jar and flips on the filtered water setting on the faucet. When I bring it to my lips, it tastes cool and delicious like it's straight out of the spring.

"Good, right?" he asks.

I nod.

"I have a well on the property, one of the few around here so that's natural spring water."

"Wow, it's some of the best water I've ever had."

"Yeah, it's one of the reasons I bought this property."

I look around the enormous open floor concept containing both the kitchen and the living room in one. There are huge skylights up above in the twenty foot ceiling, illuminating every nook and cranny. The walls are mostly bare, except for a few gigantic canvases. One is of a woman's nude body, facing away from the painter, done in an abstract style with hues of blue and violet.

"These are beautiful," I say, looking around the space.

There's a large modern chandelier the shape of an enormous hexagon hanging in the kitchen. The floors are the color of cool oak, covered with a few distressed looking rugs. Along one wall sits a modern midcentury couch and along the other is a plush chaise lounge in linen white.

"I love the way that your house is designed," I say.

"Thank you." He nods. "I did it myself."

I raise my eyebrow, surprised. It looks like something that could have a whole architectural spread in Coast magazine. I'm tempted to suggest that I pitch him and his home for the cover story.

I'm tempted, but I'm not stupid.

He's already suspicious of me and if I

bring up another story angle, I know that he won't let this go any further.

I need him to trust me. I have to put him at ease. The problem is that I feel like I'm going to pass out every time he looks at me.

"I'm sorry if I was a little rude earlier," Liam says, opening the double doors to his wide subzero refrigerator and pulling out a box of blueberries.

He raises some to my eye level and shrugs, asking, "Do you want any?"

After such a long drive, I'm feeling quite peckish and I give him a vigorous nod.

After he washes the blueberries in the sink, he transfers them to a glazed bowl with small little imperfections along the sides which makes it look like it was handmade. If the berries looked good before, now they are completely irresistible. I grab a few and pop them in my mouth.

"I'm sorry that I just showed up here. The thing is that I had no idea that you would be who I would find here. I thought that maybe D. B. Carter was actually this Matt Lipinski and he was testing me."

"You know, that wasn't really smart.

Coming out to the desert all by yourself to knock on a stranger's door. What if it had been a trick? What if he was just trying to get you to come to his house… For…"

His voice trails off, but we both know the threat that women face from strange men.

"I know, but I told my sister where I was going and I was going to stay in touch. Besides, I looked up the house and it looked quite nice."

"Yes, rich people never commit crimes," he says sarcastically and we both laugh.

"So… Can I ask you a few questions?"

He shrugs and tosses a blueberry in his mouth.

"How long have you been writing as D. B. Carter?"

"Five years or is it six? It's been a while."

"How did you get started?"

"Like any writer. I started with short stories and essays that I submitted to what feels like hundreds of literary magazines. Some got accepted, fewer got published. None made money."

"So, what happened?"

"I got sick of it. I went to this writers'

conference and I attended a talk by a fantasy writer who was self-publishing. I knew that the Kindle existed and people were doing self-publishing, but I didn't realize how successful you could be. He went over the basics of marketing, nothing too intricate, but what really caught my attention was the fact that he said that he made as much money from writing in his first year as he did from working his full-time job as a chemistry teacher. I saw that as a way to do what I really wanted to do."

"Yeah, I know that feeling," I say, nodding.

"I wanted to make a living at it. I wanted people to read my books. Before I went to the conference, I wrote a book and submitted it to forty-five different literary agents, most of whom didn't have the decency to get back to me. I figured that I had nothing to lose so I might as well just try to publish and market it myself. So, that's what I did. As soon as the first one came out, I was already done with the second and halfway through writing the third. When I did research on independent publishing, I realized that it's all about content. The readers who like these kinds of books are feverish for more titles. They just want to read them all. Well, I decided that if that's what they wanted, then that's what I'm going to give them."

"Did you sell books right away?"

"No, not at first. I took a class on Facebook advertising and then another one. Still, I struggled. But I figured that if I have content and books for people to read, then I can always tweak the marketing and the advertising and learn more about how to do it right. About a year into it, I finally hit on the right ad copy, blurb, cover combination, and people started to download my books and read them. I continued to publish and I still publish a book about every six weeks."

"Wow, that's a lot."

"Yes, it is, but the thing is that I have been trying to be a writer for my whole life so once I started being successful, I figured the best thing that I can do is keep writing."

"I like that attitude. That's probably going to take you far in life."

"Well, it took me here." He points to his

house. "I never had the goal of being rich, I just wanted my books to find readers. Then, the more books I had, the more readers I found. It was kind of like a snowball effect, but I appreciate every last one of those readers."

26

EMMA

I have never spoken to a writer before in real life and I find this conversation utterly fascinating. Of course, I have learned a little in the Facebook groups and read what feels like a hundred different writing advice books on Amazon. Yet, it feels so exhilarating to talk to one in real life. Especially, one who is so successful.

"How do you manage to publish so often?"

"Well, I have a lot of them already written and in various stages of editing and marketing. I have the pre-order set up for the next five books, but I'm already working on book six in that series."

"How long are your books?"

"About 50,000 words. 300 pages, give or take. I found that to be the sweet spot."

"Are most fantasy books much longer?"

"Yes, especially those that are traditionally published. I personally like the feeling of completing a book and then staying in the series, not just as a writer but also as a reader. There's something about finishing something that gives you this positive feeling and I want to give that to my readers."

"So, how much do you write each day? Each month?"

He pauses for a moment and looks out into the distance. I follow his gaze and we stare at the horizon where a gigantic saguaro cactus reaches for the sky.

A big black crow, or maybe a raven, perches on the top, balancing on the bright yellow bud of a flower, expertly avoiding the needles of the cactus.

"Different things and different approaches work for different writers," Liam says. "When I first started out, my goal was to just write 3000 words a day. I would often procrastinate and sometimes it would take me hours to get this done. Then I immersed myself in books about the writing process, experimenting with other writers' approaches like they are jackets in a department store. A small few were a good fit, but most did not."

"So, what happened?"

"I know that you want a straightforward answer, but you didn't ask a straightforward question. The truth is that different approaches work for different people at different parts of their life as a writer."

I nod, taking a sip of my water and wait for him to continue.

"In the beginning, I experienced a lot of writer's block because I wasn't sure where I wanted the story to go. Then I started doing a lot of meticulous outlining. I had to know exactly what was going to happen in my story in order to move forward. That cut out a lot of the planning stages while I was writing. Then, just as I figured out how to outline and plot, something strange happened. I did it enough and with enough books that I no longer needed to outline.

And if I do it too much now, know too much about my characters and the story, I end up with writer's block again."

"Really?"

"I start with who the main character or characters are and what it is they want. All primary characters have to want something otherwise the story isn't going to go anywhere. Then I know the basic midpoint and I know how the book or the series ends. So, I sit down and fill in the blanks."

"Wow, that's amazing," I say. "I have been struggling with writing this one book and have about 20,000 words, but I'm stuck. I'm tempted to try something else."

"You need to focus on achievable goals. You started this book, writing another 30,000 words isn't going to kill you. I'd recommend that you set yourself a goal, like an hour a day, and stick to it."

"What if I just sit in front of the computer and stare at the blank page?"

"No, you can't do that. You have to plan out where you're going to write. Since you don't have much experience with writing fiction, outline the whole novel. Write a paragraph about what's going to happen in the next chapter and the one after that. Then just sit down and write them."

"Is that what you did?"

"That's what I did at first," Liam says, shaking his head and running his fingers through his hair. "Then I realized that I could write a lot more a day and finish more books. I started doing sprints of twenty - thirty minutes following the Pomodoro method. I would write eight, sometimes ten hours a day, but only for a short period of time, like seven days in a row."

"So, when you were doing that, how fast could you write the book?"

"My fastest time writing a book was in five days. It was exhausting, though, and frankly, not really worth it."

"What do you mean?"

"Well, I thought that speed was the most important thing in getting the first draft out, but what happened was that I was so exhausted by the end of that first draft, and basically any draft that I did in under ten days, that I had to take a bunch of days off afterward just to recuperate. I was starting to feel burned out. Remember, I'm not just a writer, I'm also an author."

I lean back against the swivel chair and cross my legs. He looks at me with his devilish grin and runs his tongue over his lower lip.

He seems to be one of those men who doesn't quite understand exactly how attractive he is or maybe he does and he just doesn't care.

I lean forward, resting my elbows on the cool marble and ask him to explain.

"Traditionally published writers, all they have to do is write. They typically put out a book a year, if they are dedicated, and some do two books a year. It's really hard to make it as an indie author with such a small number of books. Basically, you need to build up a big catalog that people have to read through in order to make any money."

"You're not exactly scrounging by here," I say, looking around his place.

"No, I'm not, but most indie authors are not as successful as I am. I invest a lot in Facebook advertising and I invest a lot in educating myself about what's happening in the industry. I take a couple of classes a year and I also attend conferences that focus entirely on indie publishing. I talk to other authors and we discuss what's working and what's not. Mostly, I publish."

I nod and try to interject, but he continues.

"I built up a bit of a catalog so that I have some leeway in terms of my publishing. If I want to take a day off or a week off, I can. Maybe even a month. There are hungrier authors coming after me and I have seen others who have made as much as I have suddenly dwindle down to making almost nothing. If you don't have new books out, then someone else will catch your readers' attention. My readers want to read something new every two months, if not sooner. Perhaps, I can push it to three months, but if I'm only putting out two books a year, I'm going to lose them."

"Wow, that's a lot."

"I worked really hard to get here and this is the only thing I've ever wanted to do. My readers allow me to do my dream job for a living."

"I really appreciate you telling me all of this," I say. "I had no idea that this industry even existed. I mean, I knew about the Kindle, I knew that some people were self-publishing, but I had no idea that people were doing so well."

"Some people are making thirty thousand dollars per year. Others are making a six-figure salary. Then there are those that are making six figures a month, and some are making in the high six figures a month."

I shake my head and think about my salary of thirty-five thousand dollars a year.

"This sounds like a gold rush," I say.

"It's not. Actually, the gold rush is over. Back in 2011 and 2012, authors were putting their books up on Kindle and doing no advertising at all, with crappy covers and they were still clearing six figures or more. Many of them got traditional publishing deals and the majority of those said that they're not really worth it. There's just a lot more money to be made in independent publishing if you write books that the audience wants, that fit the stories that you want to tell, and if you publish those books consistently. Learning how to do Facebook advertising as well as Amazon and pop-up advertising isn't going to hurt. In fact, that's pretty much required."

"So, is that what you meant by you being an author in addition to being a writer?"

He nods and says, "When I was first starting out, the field was pretty robust and competitive, but I didn't have any money to pay a cover designer. What I would do is watch YouTube videos and figure out how to use Photoshop. I started out with some basic covers. They weren't the best, but I have republished a number of my old books and rebranded them with new covers, new blurbs, and things like that. Anyway, you learn if you take the time to learn, and time was what I had since I didn't have much money."

"What about now?"

"The funny thing is that I actually learned enough that I continue to make my own covers. I don't know exactly how to communicate what I want on the cover since I have no idea what it is that I even want. So,

I look for stock images, I manipulate them, and I look at other covers to try to find inspiration. Of course, the covers and the blurbs are your first point of contact with your readers so they have to be spot on for your category, otherwise your book will never be bought."

"Wow, you know so much about this," I say, shaking my head. "I wish I could just talk to you about this forever."

"Well, you're more than welcome to stay for dinner, but only if you promise to tell me something about yourself as well. I'm a bit of a recluse if you hadn't noticed so when I'm around people, I tend to dominate the conversation."

I laugh and agree to his terms.

27

EMMA

When we take the conversation to the couch, I ask him about how he writes now.

He has already told me more than a lot, but it seems like he mainly said what hasn't worked or what has worked in the past. Not what is working now.

"Well," Liam says, taking a sip of his tea from a glass see-through mug.

The peppermint tea is golden brown in color and there is a pyramid shaped teabag bopping at the surface.

"Why are you so curious about this?" he asks. "Is it just writer's block or is it something else?"

“It's mainly the writer’s block. I’m working on a love story, I guess a romance, and I just don't know where to take the characters. I have introduced them and they've gotten together, but now I'm stuck.”

“I don't know how to help you get out of that predicament except to say that your characters have to want something. Unlike people who go through life generally bouncing around like balls in a pinball machine, with few clearly delineated goals, characters don't have the luxury to do that.”

I swirl the little glass spoon in my see-through teacup and stare at the rip in my jeans.

“Initially, your characters’ main goal was to get together, with one another, wasn't it?”

“Yes, I guess.”

“There are other things going on. If it's a romance, then you had to bring the two of them together. There had to be a spark. There had to be a fight. There had to be some intimacy.”

I nod.

“Now? That's the spot that you're stuck at, right?”

My eyes get wide.

I can't believe that he has pinpointed the exact stopping point in a novel that he has never read or even heard of until this moment.

"So, how do I get out of that situation?"

"You have to create some tension. They've gotten together and now they need a reason to stay together. They need tension. You could break them up or add some drama to their lives. Somebody who is against them, somebody trying to push them apart. Maybe it's something external like his mother, her mother, or money. Maybe it's internal like he isn't ready for a relationship or she is not ready to be exclusive. You could throw in some misunderstandings with an ex-girlfriend, but I would caution you to use those lightly. You can't have too many misunderstandings, unless of course you are writing a comedy. Is it a comedy?"

I think back on my angst ridden, long-suffering heroine and the secretly sensitive, alpha guy that brings her to her knees.

"No," I say. "My story is definitely not a romantic comedy."

"You have to think about what's driving the story. What problems do they have and how can you amplify those problems? The biggest issue that first-time writers have, I did as well, is that the main characters tend to be perfect and flat. The best stories are those where you take a flawed character with certain motivations and goals then you throw everything you can at them. They have to go through a lot, as many obstacles as possible in order to get what they want. I think that's what my readers like best about my books."

"That's what I like about your books."

He shrugs and says, "You really don't have to lie. Not everybody likes fantasy romance and that's totally fine with me. My parents haven't even read them."

"Wow, plot twist," I say.

He laughs.

"Wait, are you serious? Your parents haven't read your books?"

"Nope. That's okay, they're not for everyone."

"Still, I thought that they would at least be interested in your work."

"You don't know my parents."

"You're so successful. How could they not…"

The thought is just shocking to me. Despite my parents' objections to my line of work, I know that they read every single article that I write and always praise me for them.

"My parents never wanted me to be a writer. They thought that it was a waste of time. I have an okay relationship with them, but it exists outside of my work. If you end up writing and polishing fiction, you'll find out that your readers exist on the Internet and out there in the world. They will likely not be found in your family. If your family members do read your book, then they will only be doing it as a favor, and that's not the sort of favor that you want."

I shake my head, some aspects of who Liam is are finally becoming clear. Yet with every question that I ask and get an answer to, five more sprout up.

"So, no one in your family has ever read your books?"

He shakes his head and starts, "Not that

I know of. I use that pen name for a reason. When I was first getting started, I wasn't sure where this was all going to go. Frankly, I was embarrassed by the fact that I was pursuing this line of work, but the more authors that I met, the more that I found out about it, how interested the readers are, and how voracious their book buying is, the more excited I got about pursuing this line of work. Publishing houses will have you believe that there's something amateurish about what we do but in reality, we work way harder than any of them."

"Why aren't more people doing this?" I ask.

"It involves a lot more than just writing. There are a lot of technical components. But also, not many traditional writers know that we get seventy percent of our royalties while they only get ten percent."

"Ten percent?"

"I don't know exactly and most publishing deals vary a little bit, but it's pretty common for writers to get ten to fifteen percent after the publisher's expenses."

"But they promote them, right?"

"No, they don't. They will of course make some general advertisements, send out a newsletter to their subscribers, and do some basic things like that, but when it comes to a real advertising campaign with real money put behind it, like the ones they do for the really big name authors, they will stop short of that."

"How do you know?"

"I had a three-book deal with one of the five biggest publishers. The first book was a book that I had already written and published. They asked me to expand it another thirty thousand words. They added a new cover and blurb to it. When they published it, they promoted it and I ended up making only three thousand dollars in three months."

"How much did you make when you published it?"

"Six thousand dollars in the first month. The whole reason that I signed a contract was that I thought they would take me to the next level. They actually took me a few pegs down. They wasted a lot of my time and told me that I couldn't release books around that time period."

"What happened?" I ask.

"I ended that relationship. It just wasn't working out. This was for a thriller brand I was testing out so it didn't impact my fantasy name at all. I didn't write the books under D. B. Carter. This was earlier in my career, about two years in when I was trying to experiment a lot with different styles and different approaches."

"Wow, that really sucks."

"Unfortunately, I'm not the only one who had that experience or something similar to that. I've talked to a number of indie authors who regret going the traditional route when they were offered advances. Most of the time the advances are quite small. Plus, you rarely make anything beyond that amount. Especially, when you're starting out. When it comes to indie publishing, if you can write books you like in a popular genre and they're good, meaning addictive, the sky is the limit."

I nod my head, taking it all in. When I first decided to come out here, I had no idea that I was going to get a lesson in how to publish a novel or rather how to become a successful author. Now, the wheels in my head start spinning. Perhaps, I can do something like this.

"Writing a novel has always been a dream of mine," I say. "Since I wasn't sure if it would ever be published, it felt like an impossible and perhaps useless hobby."

"Well, I'm here to tell you that it's not. If it's something that's in you, then you should do it. The world has never been more receptive to it. The Amazon Kindle has really changed publishing and opened it up to the world. I can't tell you how many emails I get from people who are discovering reading and the real joy of escaping into my books. I love that. I love hearing those stories because they really inspire me. Whenever I'm having a hard day, whenever I can't focus on anything, I get one of those emails and suddenly I realize what my life's purpose is. I love to write and I write mainly for myself, but the fact that I can lift my readers up and make them happy, when previously they were not, and distract them from something terrible going on in their life, that's when I really know that it's worth it."

I open my mouth to say something in response, but my mind goes blank. Somehow, his words really nail it for me.

I know exactly how he feels, even if it's just on a small level. The few messages that I have received about my articles have really made my week and made me feel like this whole writing thing isn't just me talking into an echo chamber.

"I'm surprised that you're such a recluse," I say after a moment. "I mean, you have so much to say and so many opinions about this, yet you don't really exist out there in a voice."

"What do you mean?" he asks.

"Well, you know the role these podcasts, YouTube channels, and blogs play. They're about how to write and how to publish, etc. I think that your perspective is really needed and yet it's not available."

He shrugs his shoulders and says, "I don't like to get involved."

"I know, it's outside your comfort zone, but you have a lot of valuable information to offer people. You yourself have said that you rely so much on these Facebook groups and blogs for information that others have put together in order to start your career and to keep it going."

He furrows his brow and puts his cup on the slab of granite masquerading as the coffee table.

"Is this your, not so slick, way of getting me to go on the record with you?" he asks.

28

LIAM

I haven't talked to anyone that honestly outside of a conference in a while. The people that attend those writing conferences are interested in becoming professional writers and ever since I started selling more and more books, I've realized how important it is to give back to the community.

The self-publishing/independent publishing community exists entirely as a result of successful authors telling their stories, along with the mistakes that they have made so that others can learn from them.

I don't know if Emma will actually finish

her book. Many people say that they want to be writers, but they don't actually devote themselves fully to it.

My hopes for her are high.

She's a determined journalist.

I have read a number of her stories and they are all well researched and insightful. She might make a good thriller writer.

"So, are you pretty much saying that you're not going to let me write the story?" Emma asks.

I bite my lower lip and look out of the floor-to-ceiling window that looks out onto the desert.

"I'd prefer it if you didn't," I say after a moment.

"Why?"

"I like my privacy."

"I wouldn't have to say your real name. It could just be an article about you," she suggests.

I shake my head and add, "I'd rather not."

She doesn't press it even though I know that she's disappointed.

I don't really have a good reason for

saying no to her. I have said yes to a number of writer conferences and other author events, but then again, I never used my real name. Everyone there just met me as D. B. Carter. Whatever article she would write would be about who I am as a person, where I live, and probably even sketches about my home.

I don't need that.

I can't have that.

When she tells me that she lives near downtown, I tell her that I used to live in West Hollywood.

"I lived on the second floor of a four-plex, in a one bedroom apartment."

"Did you have any roommates?"

"No," I say. "The rent was a bit cheaper then."

"What made you move out here?"

"Look around," I say, pointing at the enormous blue sky and the boulders rising out of the earth out in the distance. "I love it here. There's so much nature – ravens, eagles, coyotes, rabbits. They all come out when they think that I'm not home."

"How much land do you own?" she asks.

"Forty acres. I was planning on building a new house, but then this one showed up and I had to have it. It was beautiful and it fit my aesthetic perfectly; midcentury-modern with some inspiration of adobe."

"And back around the corner?" she asks. "Is that a pool?"

"Yes," I say. "I love swimming. I had that put in. It's not very warm now, but I also have a hot tub and there are only a few pleasures that are as wonderful as sitting in it in the middle of the night and watching the Milky Way."

I watch as she makes a quiet mmm-mmm sound, imagining it.

Her hair falls casually to her face and her eyelids grow soft. She props up her head with her hand and looks around my home.

I have transformed the dining room into a library.

I still have a dining room table there. It's sleek and low-profile with spindly midcentury modern style legs. The walls of the dining room are lined with books.

I read a lot on my iPad and Kindle, alternating between two of my favorite retailers, but there are other books that I also like to have in paperback and hardcover.

Emma points to all the books.

"I'm not much of a consumer, but when it comes to books, I don't tell myself no. As a result, if you go down to the Angel View thrift store in Yucca Valley that's sandwiched between Ralph's grocery store and a Ross department store, you'll find that they have a very robust book section and most of those books are mine. I don't keep everything I read, otherwise my three-car garage would be overflowing with them."

"You really give away all your books?"

"What else am I going to do with them? I only keep the ones that I really enjoyed or want to reread in the future. Other ones? I figure that it's best to share."

"Yeah, I agree. I love going through the collections at thrift stores. They're so different from those in bookstores."

"You'll see a lot of the popular authors, but you also get those shooting star kind of books," I say, almost finishing her thought.

She turns around and stares at me.

Our eyes meet.

I take a step forward and look down at her mouth.

She licks her lips and I try to stop myself from leaning over and just kissing her.

She waits, but I hesitate.

Then… The moment passes.

It's for the best. She is engaged to a friend of mine, or at least she was. I have plenty of my own problems, as is.

"Tell me about Alex," I say, taking a step away from her and making sure that whatever moment that has passed between us disperses for good.

As soon as I say his name, Emma withdraws into herself.

She even puts back the books that she took off the shelf and runs her finger nervously around the picture on the cover.

"What do you want to know?"

"Anything that you want to share with me," I say.

"He cheated on me and it's over, but, of course, there are lingering…"

"Doubts?" I fill in the blank.

She starts to shake her head vigorously from side to side, while saying, "Absolutely not. There are no doubts, more like sadness."

She turns her body away from me and I'm not sure what to do. I watch as her shoulders move up and down and then I realize that she's sobbing.

Without hesitating for another moment, I walk over to her and wrap my arms firmly around her.

"Shh," I whisper into her ear. "It's all going to be okay."

She shakes her head and her cries become more powerful.

She mumbles something and struggles for breath, but I can't quite make out what she's saying.

"It's going to be okay," I repeat myself over and over again.

I hold her like that for a long time until she turns around and buries her face in my shoulder.

I haven't held anyone this close since… My throat tightens and I force myself to swallow hard to keep my tears at bay.

I take a few deep breaths.

I breathe through the nose and exhale

through the mouth just like the meditation app that I forced myself to install on my phone has instructed me to do.

Slowly, I relax and that feeling that the ground is falling away from me disappears.

"Are you okay?" I ask, clearing my throat after she calms down a bit.

"I'm really sorry," she says, wiping her eyes with her palms. "I don't know what came over me. That was so… Pathetic."

"No," I say, pulling her close to me and looking into her eyes. "You've been through a really traumatic experience and you just haven't dealt with it yet."

"Alex doesn't deserve my tears."

"You are not crying for him," I say.

She looks up at me inquisitively.

"You're not crying for him," I repeat myself to make sure that she hears me. "Your tears are for the life that you have lost. You thought that you were engaged to a different man and then you found out that was a lie. That's okay. We all go through that. It's just really raw right now."

"Have you ever gone through anything like that?" Emma asks, pulling out one of the brightly colored chairs around the dining table.

She runs her fingers over the lemon yellow fabric, the exact match to the lemons growing in the backyard, and sits down.

29

LIAM

"Have you ever been through something like that?" Emma asks again.

"I've been through a lot," I say quietly.

"Like what?"

I look down at the floor. Skylar runs over and brushes along my leg, no longer seeing Emma as an enemy.

Then I look at my hands, broad and thick and tan, they used to look so different when I lived in the city.

Out here, working with my horses and taking care of the goats, the chickens, and my garden, I was forced to become a different person and my body has changed to match that.

"We don't know each other very well," I say after a long pause.

She waits for me to add a "but" to that statement, but I don't. I'm not qualifying it, not yet.

"Yes, of course," she adds when she gets the point, after an excruciatingly long pause.

I hope it doesn't change anything in our relationship, but for now I have to keep my secrets to myself.

Emma gets up and walks around the wall of bookshelves casually glancing at the spines. I sit back in the chair and watch. Most people tend to only display the serious authors on their bookshelves. There's an ego factor to it, like you want others to think that you are a better reader than you are, whatever the hell that means.

When she walks over to the middle, she sees all of the editions of my books. They fill up nearly an entire bookshelf all by themselves. When I first started, I never had author copies made.

I was proud of what I did, but I was also

embarrassed by displaying them proudly. It was almost as if I didn't think that my work measured up to the likes of John Irving, Jim Harrison, and other *serious* American men of letters.

But what makes a writer serious in the first place?

For some reason, if a male author writes about love, the book is considered serious literature but if a female does it then it's just fluff.

Well, fuck that.

Life is too short to pretend to be someone I'm not.

Millions of people around the world have devoured my work and have proudly displayed it on their bookshelves for everyone to see, so why shouldn't I do the same thing?

"I'm sorry to bring this up again," Emma asks, "but when we talked earlier about your writing method, you sort of mentioned what you used to do but not what you're currently doing. Can you tell me more about that? Like, how are you such a prolific author?"

"I realized that I was suffering from burnout when I started to spend a lot of hours out of my day procrastinating. So, I started to research procrastination and productivity. Then I developed a system of writing basically only for an hour a day. I can write for a lot more hours, but I limit myself to one hour exactly. Usually, spread over three writing sprints."

"Wait, that's all? So, how does that work? I thought you would be writing like six hours a day, seven days a week."

I laugh and say, "Close, but no. I now write one hour a day five out of the seven days a week. Sometimes, I will do more if I'm in the mood, but most of the time I don't."

"So, you do writing sprints?"

"Yes, twenty-five minute, twenty minute, and fifteen minute writing sprints. I tell myself that I know exactly what I need to cover or where I'm headed in the story. Then I just grab my phone and start dictating."

"You dictate?"

"It's faster than typing and I've had

issues with carpal tunnel and other wrist problems."

"How does it work?"

"I sit at my desk and talk into my phone. Sometimes I go on a walk and occasionally, I ride my horse."

Emma raises her eyebrows in utter shock, but musters to say, "I feel like you live on some other planet."

I laugh and she laughs along with me. When my hand touches her, accidentally, I don't recoil back and neither does she.

Instead she looks up at me and I lean closer to her.

The gravitational pull that I feel toward her is impossible to deny.

Now that I know that her relationship with Alex is completely over, I don't stop myself.

Our lips touch.

Her mouth is soft and delicate, but our kiss is not. There's a hunger in our kiss and I push her against the bookcase.

I haven't known her long and yet the sexual tension seems to have existed between us long before we met.

I run my fingers up her curvy body. She pulls away, but only for second and then presses harder against me.

I open my mouth slightly and let my tongue find hers. I hold her with both hands.

She kisses me back, harder each time. I push her back against the bookcase more firmly and a few books fall down on top of us.

"Oh my God!" she yelps from surprise.

I laugh and she laughs, too.

When our eyes meet again, she reaches up to kiss me, but I pull away.

"What's wrong?" she asks.

I can hear the disappointment in her voice.

"It's hard to explain," I say quietly.

"You're a writer," she says.

"I know."

I divert my eyes from her.

I know that if I were to look into them again, she would immediately know the truth about me and every last one of my secrets would be exposed.

"Okay," she says, straightening her

clothes even though they're not out of shape. "I understand."

She turns around and walks away from me. It takes me a moment to catch up to her, but when I do, I see that she's hiding her face from me.

"Emma, please stop…" I start to say. I pull her hand, but she pulls it away from me. "This isn't about you. None of this is about you."

"Of course, nothing is ever about me," she says.

I search her face, but it's blank. Whatever she's feeling, she's bottling up deep inside and all I see is a wall of anger and disappointment.

"I really like you," I say.

She doesn't know this, but even saying those words are quite difficult for me.

"Look, I know that I was engaged to your friend and that none of this should be happening between us. I'm not with him anymore so I'm not breaking any rules, but you do have your guy code."

"Alex and I are *not* friends. He invited me to your engagement party because he wanted me to invest my money with his fund. We haven't been in touch for years. I just happened to run into him."

"You haven't talked to him?"

"No, and I suspect that he didn't really have much interest in me until we talked about my investment."

"I can't believe that he invited you to our party to make a business deal."

"You can't?" I ask.

"No," she says, raising her eyebrows and shaking her head. "Of course, I *can*. Work is the only thing that he really cares about."

"Look, this has nothing to do with Alex. I like kissing you," I say, "but my life… It's complicated."

"What are you talking about?"

"I can't tell you. You found out one aspect of my life, but I have others. Things are dangerous for me. I can't say much more than that."

She stares at me, furrowing her brow.

I look at the crinkle that it makes on her forehead and realize that this is the most beautiful thing I've ever seen.

She wants to know everything, not just as a reporter but as a woman.

She deserves to be with someone who can tell her those things. Only problem is that I'm not one of those people.

"I'm going to go," Emma says.

The tone of her voice gets very low, signifying that she means business.

"Please, don't. I thought you were going to stay for dinner?"

"No, I don't think that's a good idea."

I ask her to stay again, but again she refuses. I ruined it.

She walks out the front door and slams it shut behind her. I want to follow her out and ask her to stay again, but I hesitate.

I know that it's best for her if she goes.

I'm a dangerous man with a dangerous past.

I'm not just a writer, I have demons hunting me.

More than demons, actual bad men with guns who are determined to get their revenge.

The best thing that I can do is to let her go because I know what happens if I don't. I have lost one person in my life to them, I can't have anymore innocent bystanders paying for my crimes.

I look over to the window and watch her get into her car. More than anything, I want to run out there and ask her to stay.

30

EMMA

I don't know what happened. He kissed me and I felt that he wanted me. I knew that he did and I wanted him, too.

Our mouths found each other and, suddenly, it all made sense. Then things changed.

He pushed me away. He tried to pretend that he didn't, but the trance of being there in his arms had dispersed.

I run down the steps to my car with angry tears in my eyes. I'm such a fool.

How could I let that happen?

My anger has nothing to do with Alex. I

know that I don't owe him anything and we are no longer together.

I've done nothing wrong. Still, my anger remains.

I hate that I have put myself into this situation.

Why?

The events of the whole day mash together in my mind. I have come here looking for D. B. Carter, knowing full well that the guy on that forum was lying or at least making fun of me.

Then, I happen to actually find the real D. B. Carter, who turned out to be someone I had already met.

Liam promised that he was not the guy from the forum who pointed me in this direction, but how could he *not* be?

I get into my car and shut the door. I take a few deep breaths and look in the rearview mirror. He is standing on the porch but doesn't make a step to follow me.

I let out a sigh of relief.

I don't want him. He told me all about his writing and it felt like he was opening up to me, but in reality, he's as shut as a clam.

He's unreachable and I don't need that in my life.

When I look back in the rearview mirror again, my body longs for him. It's a silly expression, one typical of books, and yet that's exactly how I feel.

Every part of me, down to the molecular and cellular level, craves him.

I shouldn't compare, but kissing Liam was nothing like kissing Alex. With Alex, things were simple. I knew that he liked me. I knew where we stood. I liked that certainty.

In the end? In the end he broke my heart in a way that will probably take me months if not years to recover.

Is this what is really going on?

Do I just want Liam because I can't have Alex?

I inhale deeply and exhale slowly through the mouth. I feel the breath escape my lips and I run my tongue over my lower lip, pausing briefly over each indentation.

Out here under the bright desert sun where the humidity is below ten percent, my lips are chapped and dry.

I lick them again to give them some

moisture and then wipe a rogue tear running down my cheek.

I press the start button on my car, but the engine doesn't start. I look at the screen thinking that I had left the key somewhere in his house, but the missing key notification doesn't pop up.

I feel around my purse and find it in there.

I press the pedal and the start button again. Again, nothing happens.

What the hell am I supposed to do now?

I try again and again, but still nothing happens. A sudden knock on the driver's window startles me and I jump.

It's Liam.

He moves slightly out of the way when I crack the door.

"My car won't start," I say.

Even though it's spring and I can feel a breeze of cool air settling on the valley, the sun is still beating down hard on the earth. Without air conditioning, the inside of the car becomes unbearable.

I step out, leaning my body against the powder blue door.

"I'm sorry," Liam says.

I ignore him and instead bury my head in my phone.

"I'm going to call AAA," I explain.

He leans over and brushes his fingertips against mine. A shock of electricity runs up my arm. When I look up at him, he takes my hand in his and squeezes it tightly.

"I'm sorry," he says with his eyes twinkling in the sunlight.

"It doesn't–"

He kisses me.

He takes a step forward and pushes my body against the car. When we collide with one another, the world falls apart and is put together again with all the pieces that make sense.

He runs his fingers slowly up the nape of my neck, reaching all the way up to my earlobes and then cradling my chin as if it were a saucer. His lips are firm and determined. At first, he was hesitant, but now he takes control.

I haven't seen this side of him before, but I like it.

I kiss him back, gently touching my

tongue with his, but when he pulls away slightly and then kisses me again, his mouth gets feverish.

His hands move up and down my body from the small of my back all the way up my spine.

After a few moments, they move toward my waist and then he cups one of my breasts.

"You're so beautiful," he says through his kisses.

Our bodies become heated, dirty, messy, and wonderful all at the same time.

When I toss my head back, he kisses down my neck to the top of my breasts. My breathing speeds up and my body starts to quiver.

I look up at the cloudless blue sky as he tugs at my jacket. The buttons seem to come out of the loops all on their own and he slides his hand under my loose-fitting blouse.

It's a peasant top that keeps my breasts slightly separated and away from him. I look down and he looks up at me, silently asking permission.

I smile and wait for him to act. It's all the

consent that he needs and he slides his hand firmly under my bra.

His body reacts against mine. I feel the hardness of it. It's almost as if it's made out of marble.

Beautiful on the outside and yet hard and imposing when up close.

The muscles in his stomach contract and retract with each breath, forming that elusive six pack and then disappearing all in a mere moment.

I run my fingers up and down the washboard abs, noticing how big he seems in comparison to me.

I'm not very tall and I'm not very thin, yet he towers over me.

Continuing to kiss me, he pulls down on my blouse exposing my breast. He takes my nipple expertly between his lips and kisses it gently. I run my hand over his belt buckle and down his pants.

His body is firm against mine so I don't quite touch it, but I can feel its outline and it's huge. The biggest I've ever felt with a nice curve to it, veering slightly to the left.

When his hands make their way down

past my panties to my core, I open my legs. I want him to feel how much I want him.

"I want you more than I've ever wanted anyone," he whispers into my ear. "I've wanted you since the first time I spotted you on the patio."

"That's because you thought that I was taken," I joke.

He pulls his lips away from mine, meets my eyes, and shakes his head.

"No, absolutely not. There's something different about you, Emma. It scares me."

When he swallows hard, I see the outline of his Adam's apple dip up and down.

I know what he means. I feel the same way.

We lose ourselves in each other's eyes for a moment, unwilling to even blink out of fear of allowing reality to rush back.

"I want you," he says.

I reach over and put my lips on his.

"Although." He pulls away slightly and presses his index finger to my lips. "I want you for more than just this moment."

"What do you mean?" I ask, kissing his finger.

"I want you to spend the week with me, here."

"I can't stay that long," I say and try to kiss him again. "I don't even think I can stay the night. I have to get back to work by Monday."

31

EMMA

His face clenches and his jaw tightens. There's a tension there that is hard to explain, but I can tell that he wants me still just as much as I want him.

"Invite me inside," I say. "I want to see your bedroom."

He hesitates.

My heart sinks.

Is this happening *again*? Did I just put myself out there just to get crushed once again?

Pulling his hands out of my panties, he withdraws into himself and buckles his jeans.

I adjust my clothing and take a deep breath to try to calm my nerves. I can't believe that he's doing this to me.

Rejecting me like this.

I know that he wants me, so why are we playing these games?

"You want something from me," Liam says, with his dark hair falling into his eyes. "I want something from you."

"I have no idea what you're talking about," I say.

"You want me to agree to that article about D. B. Carter. You want me to expose who I really am and the only way that I'll do it is if you agree to spend a week with me here."

I shake my head and cross my arms. I try to walk away from him, but he grabs my hand.

"I'm not going to sleep with you for a story," I snap at him. "I was going to sleep with you now, but I'm not going to do it like that. Not as a deal."

"I'm sorry. I don't mean to offend you. I know that you're a journalist and that you have high standards. I just want to spend time with you. I don't want you to leave, not quite yet and not for good. So, if you come here for a week, you can see how I work, we can spend time together, and anything else that happens is entirely up to you."

Now it's my turn to swallow hard, but I mutter out, "Why do you want this?"

"I want you."

"So, why did we stop?"

"I want to make you wait," he says after a very long pause.

His eyes twinkle in the sunlight and his words hit me so hard they practically blow me back.

Did I just hear him say what I think he said?

"Are you teasing me?"

"More than that. I know that you want me," he says, focusing his eyes arrogantly on mine.

"You want me, too," I say.

"There's no denying that," he says, shaking his head. "As I said earlier, I want you more than I ever wanted anyone, but that's what scares me."

"What?"

"You walked into my life and suddenly I feel upside down. Everything that used to make sense doesn't. What scares me most now is the fact that you will walk out of it just as suddenly as you came into it. That's why I want to make this deal."

I swallow hard.

"You spend one week here and I will let you write an article about me. You can call it research or you can call it whatever you want."

I look him up and down as he towers over me like a marble statue of a Greek God. Dark and lean with the slim build of a cowboy or distance runner, his face is only now getting some lines in his forehead and around his eyes. He tilts his head to one side, popping his chin out, confidently waiting for my answer.

I hate the cockiness. I hate that he's trying to make me make a decision when I don't have a choice.

Doesn't he know that my life is on the line for this?

Doesn't he know that if I don't bring the story back to my boss then everything that I have worked for is going to be taken from me?

"I don't like games."

"This isn't a game."

"Yes, it is. You're putting me into a terrible position. You're trying to pressure me. That's not what people who want to spend time with someone do. If you wanted me to spend the night, you could've just asked me. If you wanted me to spend a week with you and for us to get to know each other more, you could've asked."

"I'm asking now."

"No, you're not."

"You would've said no."

"Perhaps, but now we will never know."

Liam crosses his arms with a satisfied grin on his face. For some reason, he seems unfazed and that makes me feel even more out of control and angrier at him.

Why did he have to take this beautiful moment that we just had and turn it into something else?

We could have had some glorious sex on the hood of my car and that could've been it.

Then it occurs to me.

He wants more than that.

He wants more than a one-night stand.

"Is that what's really going on here?" I ask. "You want more than just some meaningless sex?"

"I don't want *any* meaningless sex," he says quietly. "Not with you. I want you more than anything, right now, on the roof of that car. I want to rip off your clothes, spread your legs, and push myself deep inside of you. I want to do it over and over again until you scream my name so loud that the crows on those cacti five acres away get scared and fly away. I also want more than that. I want you. All of you. For a week. In return, I will give you what you want, anything you want."

THANK you so much for reading ALL THE LIES!

I hope you are enjoying Emma and Liam's story. Can't wait to find out what happens next? Their story continues in the next book.

Read ALL THE SECRETS now!

The only way he'll agree to the story about the great and reclusive writer, D. B. Carter is if I agree to spend the week with him.

He thinks that the reason that I left is that I don't want him. Nothing could be from the truth.

He thinks I was insulted. He's wrong.

I have a fire in my body that burns just for him.

Still, I leave.

He shouldn't have asked for something like that. All that it did was push me away.

But I have to write this story to save my job.

It won't be published for a while and I'll have time to convince him to go on the record.

At least, that's what I think.

But then the article comes out and he shows up at my house.

He's angry.

I'm mad.

What happens when that fire between us starts to ignite?

What happens when he pulls me close and doesn't let go?

Read ALL THE SECRETS now!

CAN'T WAIT and want to dive into another EPIC romance right away?

Read THE PERFECT STRANGER now!

When he burst into my life, he set everything on fire.

He is a multi-millionaire, escaped inmate serving life in prison for a double murder he didn't commit.

He was once my only friend and my first crush.

He doesn't ask for help and I don't offer.

His hair falls into his face and a

strand brushes along his chiseled jaw. His vulnerability is disarming.

We both know that he shouldn't be here, but when I stare into his piercing, intense eyes, I can't look away.

I want to tell him to leave, but then he leans over and runs his finger over my lower lip.

When our mouths touch, I know that I won't be able to stop.

What happens when one night isn't enough?

Read THE PERFECT STRANGER now!

CONNECT WITH CHARLOTTE BYRD

Sign up for my **newsletter** to find out when I have new books!

You can also join my Facebook group, **Charlotte Byrd's Reader Club**, for exclusive giveaways and sneak peaks of future books.

I appreciate you sharing my books and telling your friends about them. Reviews help readers find my books! Please leave a review on your favorite site.

Sign up for my newsletter: https://www.subscribepage.com/byrdVIPList

Join my Facebook Group: https://www.facebook.com/groups/276340079439433/

Bonus Points: Follow me on BookBub and Goodreads!

ABOUT CHARLOTTE BYRD

Charlotte Byrd is the bestselling author of romantic suspense novels. She has sold over 600,000 books and has been translated into five languages.

She lives near Palm Springs, California with her husband, son, and a toy Australian Shepherd. Charlotte is addicted to books and Netflix and she loves hot weather and crystal blue water.

Write her here:

charlotte@charlotte-byrd.com

Check out her books here:

www.charlotte-byrd.com

Connect with her here:

www.facebook.com/charlottebyrdbooks

www.instagram.com/charlottebyrdbooks

www.twitter.com/byrdauthor

Sign up for my newsletter: https://www.subscribepage.com/byrdVIPList

Join my Facebook Group: https://www.facebook.com/groups/276340079439433/

Bonus Points: Follow me on BookBub and Goodreads!

facebook.com/charlottebyrdbooks
twitter.com/byrdauthor
instagram.com/charlottebyrdbooks
bookbub.com/profile/charlotte-byrd

ALSO BY CHARLOTTE BYRD

All books are available at ALL major retailers! If you can't find it, please email me at charlotte@charlotte-byrd.com

The Perfect Stranger Series

The Perfect Stranger

The Perfect Cover

The Perfect Lie

The Perfect Life

The Perfect Getaway

The Perfect Couple

All the Lies Series

All the Lies

All the Secrets

All the Doubts

All the Truths

All the Promises

All the Hopes

Tell me Series

Tell Me to Stop

Tell Me to Go

Tell Me to Stay

Tell Me to Run

Tell Me to Fight

Tell Me to Lie

Wedlocked Trilogy

Dangerous Engagement

Lethal Wedding

Fatal Wedding

Tangled Series

Tangled up in Ice

Tangled up in Pain

Tangled up in Lace

Tangled up in Hate

Tangled up in Love

Black Series

Black Edge

Black Rules

Black Bounds

Black Contract

Black Limit

Not into you Duet

Not into you

Still not into you

Lavish Trilogy

Lavish Lies

Lavish Betrayal

Lavish Obsession

Standalone Novels

Dressing Mr. Dalton

Debt

Offer

Unknown

CPSIA information can be obtained
at www.ICGtesting.com
Printed in the USA
LVHW040210161022
730798LV00025B/626

9 781632 251671